CALAMITY AT THE CARNIVAL

FIREFLY JUNCTION COZY MYSTERY #5

LONDON LOVETT

WILD FOX PRESS

CHAPTER 1

$\mathcal{I}$t was one of those halfway slumbers. I was aware of my surroundings but my eyelids were heavy and my head was in a drowsy fog. The tickle on my nose was all too real.

With a heavy hand, I swiped at my face without opening my eyes. The tickle returned, only more insistent and annoying. I crinkled my nose and waved my hand at my face again. The tickle persisted. My eyes popped open and I sat up straight from my slump on the couch. The pillow I'd been clutching, like my old teddy bear friend, Chub-chub, fell to the floor.

Edward, my housemate, if one could call a two century old ghost a housemate, was hovering in front of me. The only part of the vision that was solid and not transparent was the feather in his long, white fingers.

I rubbed my nose again, not because of the tickle but to brush away the idea that a dirty feather had been so close to my mouth. "Were you touching me with that? Yuck."

Edward lifted the feather and scrutinized it with his bold blue eyes. They were incredibly expressive for a pair of dead eyes. "Not a yuck. A pigeon, I think. It was sitting on the porch."

"That's what I figured, which is why I said yuck. It's not a bird species, it's another word for disgusting. You don't know where that feather has been," I said, recycling one of my mom's favorite warnings.

Edward waved the feather. "My best guess is that it's been sitting in a pigeon's rear end."

"My point exactly. Besides, I was awake. I was just resting my eyes."

"Then you snore while you're awake." He floated across to the window of the sitting parlor and stared outside. "It's still early in the day, but you're falling asleep because you stayed out too late with that unkempt man and his wild hair."

"It's not wild, it's thick," I countered. I stood from the couch and pounded the hug marks out of the pillow I'd been clutching.

"Thick," he scoffed. "My hair is thick, and you don't see me floating around as if I've been walking through a windstorm."

"That's because your hair is permanently tied back in a blue ribbon. And before you even suggest it, that same blue ribbon would definitely not work today. Let's just say, the men's hair ribbon fad fizzled out a few years back."

I could tell by the fading in and out of his features, something that happened when his ghostly emotions were running high, that we were not finished with the discussion.

Edward tossed the feather into the hearth. The sitting parlor was one of the first rooms to be completely restored. It had a carved marble mantle that I loved and that gave the room terrific character. Edward's dislike of my original color choice, Cupid Pink, was what had prodded him to reveal his existence to me. It was a day I will never, ever forget.

"He keeps you out far too long. It's not right," Edward harrumphed in his posh accent.

I stopped to pick up the three tennis balls Newman had left in the room. "I'm perfectly safe with Jackson. As I've told you many times—he's a detective."

Edward laughed dryly. "That's supposed to ease my mind?" he asked. "In my day, I knew constables who were even more dissolute than the criminals they chased."

I decided not to respond. Edward's memory was still anchored firmly to the early nineteenth century. I'd learned it was futile and a waste of energy to try and change his opinion about the ways of the world.

My dog, suddenly alerted that someone was moving his precious tennis balls, came bounding into the room. I tossed the three balls out into the hallway, and he skittered after them.

"You have no chaperone," Edward continued. "If I could leave this—this prison—I'd go along on your outings to make sure he doesn't take advantage of you."

We'd had the same argument so often, it normally just amused me, but this morning, his words tugged at my chest. I smiled and walked toward him. His face came more into focus. Incorporeal or not, the man presented a dashing image.

"I'm perfectly safe with Jackson, but thank you for worrying, Edward."

His face dipped so I couldn't see his expression clearly. "You're welcome," he said quietly.

I turned to leave.

"After all, someone has to. It's obvious your own judgment is clouded when it comes to this man."

I threw up my arms. "There you go obliterating our moment."

"What moment?" He floated after me as I left the room.

"You and I were having a heartfelt moment back there, but instead of leaving it at 'you're welcome', you had to keep blathering on."

"I don't blather. I just reason things out. By the way, you should probably look at that silly metal tablet you're always staring at. It's been buzzing like an angry hive of bees ever since you fell—fell *awake* on the couch," he quipped.

Instinctively, I patted the pocket on my sweatshirt, but there was no phone. "I must have left it in the kitchen."

I hurried down the hallway. My phone was sitting on the table next to my half empty coffee cup. Jackson and I had gone out to a movie and dinner. Then I'd made the mistake of reading a book until two in the morning. I got up early but felt so tired, I decided to take a quick nap. According to the clock on the wall, that quick nap had lasted a good hour and a half.

I grabbed my phone and flicked my thumb across the screen. There were four voice mails. I quickly pressed the star key to listen to them.

Edward was at the window. "I think your sister is in pain. She has a contorted look on her face."

I tossed the phone back on the table and raced to the window. Lana was trudging toward the house with her right arm wrapped in a bag of frozen peas. "She must have hurt herself." My heart pounded as I raced to the entry.

Lana was just climbing the front steps as I swung open the door. "What happened?" I asked.

Lana shook her head. Her face was pale. Even her lips looked white. "Just darn bad luck. I was on a stepladder trying to pull down a box of lights, and my foot slipped off. How come you didn't answer your phone?"

"I'm sorry. I didn't hear it." I helped her inside. "Did you hurt your arm?" I asked, motioning toward the bag of frozen peas.

"I think so." She winced and held her breath as she lifted the makeshift ice pack. Her slim wrist was red from the icy bag. It definitely looked different than normal. She held both arms out for comparison. "I guess the S shape at the wrist is not supposed to be there."

I felt the color from my face drain as I stared down at her

warped arm. "I don't think we need an x-ray machine to diagnose that as a broken wrist. You poor thing, it must hurt badly."

"Surprisingly, I can't feel too much, even my fingers are numb. But I don't think that's from the peas."

"I'll get my coat and keys so I can drive you to the clinic." I rushed down the hallway and past a concerned looking ghost to the kitchen. "Do you need something?" I called to my sister. "Aspirin or a cup of water?"

"No, thanks." Lana was at the kitchen entrance. "Let's not tell Emi and Nick. They only just left for their romantic stay at the bed and breakfast. If we tell them, they'll probably turn right around."

"I agree." I tapped the side of my head. "That's right. You and I are taking care of the animals."

Lana lifted up one side of her lip. "I might still be able to toss a bit of scratch out for the chickens."

I pulled on my coat. "Nonsense. You're going to need to rest. I'll take care of the farm."

She stood there with the same apologetic grin. "And how do you feel about filling a hundred goodie bags for a sweet sixteen party?"

"I forgot you had a big party next weekend." Lana's event planning business had taken off like a rocket, and it seemed she was always swamped with work. A broken wrist, especially a right wrist, was going to set her back. The last thing she needed was to fret about the business. "Don't worry, Raine and I will make sure everything gets finished."

We headed to the door.

"How are you going to take care of the farm, help out my business and work on the newspaper, all at the same time?" she asked with perfectly reasonable skepticism.

"I'll take vitamins and drink a lot of coffee." The late spring morning had started out with a few clouds, but the sky had cleared to a bright blue. I held my hand under her elbow to help her down the steps.

"Sunni, I broke my wrist, not my hip. I can walk on my own."

"Guess you're lucky it was only your wrist. I know I've said this to the point of irritation, but you need to hire more help. Your business is blooming, but you're still trying to do it all on your own and Raine can only help out when she's not busy with her own business."

"I know, and yes, it has been to the point of irritation. But you're right." We stopped at my jeep. Lana stared at the step to climb up into the passenger seat. It wasn't going to be an easy task with one arm. "You need a much lower car for emergency runs to the doctor."

I helped her into the jeep and buckled her seatbelt. "Let's just hope this emergency run thing doesn't become a habit."

CHAPTER 2

I waited for Jackson on the front porch, deciding it was always better to keep him out of the house. Edward had complained about me staying out late with Jackson the night before, so I was certain I could expect shenanigans from my live-in ghost. Edward had already made it clear how he felt about Jackson, and I didn't need the aggravation. Whenever Edward was upset, he tended to forget that I was the only person who was *privileged* enough to hear and see him. More than once, the persistent noise that my contractors, Ursula and Henry Rice, made in the house, had driven him to get sloppy and nearly expose his existence. At Christmas, he'd gone so far as to rip a hammer from Ursula's hand, an antic that nearly cost me my contractors. It had taken a good two weeks before Henry could talk his sister into working at the inn again. And in those two weeks, I'd made it crystal clear to Edward that he had to stay well away from the pair. Henry and Ursula had been back a few months. So far, the truce was holding firm. The Rice siblings were making good progress on the restoration project, and my easily annoyed spirit was behaving.

Jackson had pulled on a black baseball cap. His thick hair stuck jutted out in every direction. He stopped in front of the porch and pointed down at his brown leather cowboy boots. "Did you call for a cowboy, little lady?" He pulled off his cap. "I'm ready for my farm chores. Just point me toward the hungry chickens."

"Shouldn't that hat you're holding be in the shape of a Stetson? I do like a nice black cowboy hat." I bounded down the steps to him.

He pulled me close for a quick kiss, then peered down at me with his amber gaze. "Sorry, the boots are the closest thing I've got to cowboy gear." He released me. "How is your sister?"

"Loopy from the painkillers, but the doctor said he thinks six weeks in a cast should do the trick. No surgery."

"That's good to hear." We headed to his car and got inside. "I thought we could check out the spring carnival after we get done feeding the animals. I hear they're serving deep fried cupcakes on a stick this year."

"Nothing about that sounds right. Cupcakes belong on cute little doily covered plates and not on a stick or anywhere near a deep fryer, for that matter. But I won't say no to cotton candy."

"Well, as long as you're going for the healthy option." Jackson pulled onto the road for the brief drive to Emily's farm.

"I missed the carnival last year. Lana mentioned it's a yearly thing," I said.

"Every year when the kids are on spring break, the Stockton Traveling Carnival rolls into town. I've been going since I was a wee little guy."

I laughed. "I can't imagine you were ever small enough to be called *wee*, but I'll bet you were cute and rascally."

"I was definitely a rascal." He pulled onto the gravel path leading to the chicken farm. "Just don't expect to be too wowed by the carnival. You know how when you're little and a carnival and amusement park seems like a gigantic, magical universe with scream-worthy rides, games offering cool prizes and sugary treats as far as the eye can see?"

I nodded. "Yes, and when those kid glasses with the magical filters come off, you see a run-down, shabby collection of rides that look underwhelming and unsafe, games where it takes defying all rules of physics to win the big teddy bear on the wall and treats that make your stomach head back to the car in surrender. I'm familiar with the phenomenon. It's called 'everything looks way better when you're a kid'."

He laughed as he parked the car just outside of the chicken coop area. Busy hens of every color, shape and size scratched at the ground in front of the whimsically painted nesting houses.

Jackson turned to me. "We don't have to go to the carnival."

"No, let's go. It'll be fun. It's been a long time since I've sat on the sticky seat of a carnival ride."

We climbed out of the car. "Which do you prefer, chickens or horses and goats?" I asked.

The hens saw us nearing the coop and began a thunderous chorus of hysterical chicken sounds.

"Uh, I think I'm more of a horse and goat person," Jackson said. "I'll let you handle that enthusiastic flock."

"All right. The hay is inside the green door in the barn. Make sure they all have water. Oh, and don't forget to muck." I smiled.

"Guess it makes sense that mucking is part of the deal," he said. "Good thing I'm wearing my boots."

I took a moment to watch him lumber away on his long legs. His flannel shirt was stretched tightly across his back, and the black boots made him even taller. I sighed quietly. For the first few months of our relationship, I'd cautioned myself not to fall head over heels for Jackson. Feet always on the ground, Sunni, I'd chanted more than once. But it was pretty hard to keep two feet on the ground around Detective Brady Jackson. Gravity just didn't seem to work right when he was near.

Merely lifting the lid on the can, where the buckets of feed were stored, sent the flock into a frenzy. I'd fed the chickens several times but usually under Emily's watchful eye. I was slightly reluctant to walk into the hen yard with my bucket full of grain. I glanced back toward the barn. Jackson had disappeared inside, so it was too late to switch jobs. He was in there getting nuzzled by sweet goats, while I was walking into an angry, anxious mob with sharp beaks and attitudes. Some of the bigger hens were elbowing, (without the actual elbows) through the crowd to get first crack at the frightened woman with the feed bucket. A terrifying memory flashed through my head of a ten-year-old Sunni walking excitedly to the dolphin feeding pool at Marine World, only to have the paper plate of dead sardines ripped from her hand by rude seagulls long before she reached the dolphins.

I took a deep breath and lifted my chin to feign a tiny shred of confidence and pushed through the outer gate. One more gate and I'd be inside the yard, lost in a hurricane of feathers and clucking. I pushed my chin a little higher. Another terrifying memory entered my head, this time of a twelve-year-old Sunni wearing her new pink tennis shoes and a bright smile, happily tossing bread crumbs at a duck pond, only to be chased helter skelter across the park by a giant goose determined to have every last bread crumb to herself. In a panic, I threw the entire bread bag at the giant gray menace and ran for the girls' restroom, certain she wouldn't follow me inside.

A group of hens circled the gate now, quietly clucking to each other as if plotting some kind of diabolical plan.

"You can do this," I said and silently cursed Lana for picking this weekend to break her wrist.

The girls spread out as I pushed open the gate but then quickly swept back in toward me. I frantically tossed grain about the yard to get them away from my legs. Minutes later, the flock of hens had quieted down and scattered around the yard to peck up the goodies. I was feeling quite proud of my accomplishment and far more relaxed when a beak pecked so hard at my calf, I felt it through my jeans.

I spun around and found myself staring into the menacing gaze of King Harold, the one and only rooster on the farm. Emily rarely let him into the coop. She must have worried he wouldn't be safe outside of the fencing while they were away.

"King Harold." I lowered the bucket to use as a shield between us. "Nice to see you." I hoped the bird didn't hear the nervous tremor in my voice. I reached into the bucket. "How about I give you the last bits of grain and then you let me walk, without incident, back to the gate?"

King Harold stared at me with laser beam eyes. He seemed to be contemplating my offer.

I smiled politely and tossed the broken bits of corn his direction, then I walked a wide berth around him. He ignored the food and raced after me like a rabid beast.

I screamed and raced toward the gate. The latch was stuck. I turned around and threw the bucket at King Harold. He easily dodged it and lunged toward me, claws in the air. The gate latch finally opened. I slipped through and shut the gate hard behind me. I turned around to stick my tongue out at the King before spinning triumphantly back to the outside gate.

Jackson was just putting away his phone.

"Did you just film that?" I asked.

His mouth slanted into a sly smile. "Maybe." He pulled a note out of his pocket. "Found this in the barn. It's from Emily." He unfolded it and read it aloud. "Be careful when you go into the chicken yard. I put King Harold in with the hens."

"My sister—always thinks of everything," I said with a head shake. I glanced back at the chicken yard. King Harold was strutting along the chicken coop wire with his bright red comb held high like a crown.

"I think he won that round," Jackson noted.

"Yes. I think his royal title has gone to his head." I sighed. "The next three days should be quite the adventure."

CHAPTER 3

The week long carnival had been set up on a vast expanse of land just off Butternut Crest between Firefly Junction and Hickory Flats. It butted up against a wilderness park area that offered hook-ups and restrooms for travelers. The vacation spot was filled with motorhomes, large box trucks and three eighteen wheelers, two that were flatbeds, and each showcasing the Stockton Carnival logo on their cabs. A group of tents had been propped up on a section of grass outside the park bathrooms.

"That is not an easy lifestyle," I said. "Living in trailers and showering in park restrooms. Then there's the whole packing up and moving every few weeks. I hate the task of putting groceries away. I can't imagine having to pack up an entire carnival just to pull everything back off the truck a few days later."

"I don't know—" Jackson said. "As a kid, I dreamt of living the life of a traveling carnie." We headed toward the entrance. "Going from place to place, eating nothing but fried, sugary junk food with no one telling you what to do."

I laughed. "If the employees eat only carnival food, then I'd say the life expectancy of a carnie is thirty, thirty-five at the most."

Jackson paid the admission fee and we walked under the big sign boasting that we were entering what was once voted 'the number one traveling carnival'. I wondered exactly what year that vote was cast. It was easy to see that at one point in time the Stockton Traveling Carnival had been a vibrant, lively collection of tents, neon lit game booths, inviting food kiosks and thrilling rides. But the teal and pink striped canvas on the tents and awnings had faded to a dull blue and washed-out rose color. Neon signs with sporadic broken light bulbs towered over booths that were all sadly in need of more paint . . . or at the very least—less rust. The obligatory ride with the long octopus arms that floated up and down while spinning screaming riders into a wave of nausea looked particularly rickety and made a terrible screeching sound as it lifted its *tentacles* into the air.

It was Sunday, and the first full day for the carnival. The kids in Firefly Junction and the surrounding towns were on spring break, and considering the crowds swarming the booths and rides, it seemed the carnival owner was going to make a nice profit, despite the shabbiness.

Jackson stopped and stared up at the Ferris wheel that was slowly filling up with riders. "My friends and I used to really like this ride. Looks much smaller now."

"Ferris wheel, eh? I pegged you more as the hammerhead kind of guy, much more dangerous and scary. You know the kind of ride that makes you think you're going to pass out or puke or both." I squinted up to the top of the wheel where a teenage boy was rocking the bucket just enough to make his female riding mate scream with terror. She clutched at him in fear.

Jackson winked at me. "That's why we favored the Ferris wheel. I see old traditions never die."

We continued on. I took hold of his arm. "You don't expect me to believe that Brady Jackson had to resort to scare tactics to get girls to cling to him."

"Occasionally, but only when a snap of my fingers failed," he said wryly. He stopped at a basketball throw where the grand prize was a plastic blow up alien. "I used to be pretty good at this game. Shall I win you an alien? Or are you more the fuzzy unicorn type?" He pointed across to the baseball toss where a thin kid in a pink and teal striped shirt was using a megaphone to draw customers to his booth. Even the striped uniforms of the carnies looked as if they were from a bygone era, one where laundry was scrubbed on a washboard.

"Baseball is also a specialty of mine," Jackson boasted.

"Oh really? Well, I'm pretty darn good at it too. Maybe I should win *you* a fuzzy unicorn," I suggested.

"That's right, you were a softball star in high school. Do you think you can knock down all the bottles with one pitch?" he asked.

"Haven't played in a few years but I think I've still got it." We headed toward the baseball game. We passed the dark green tent that boasted ten dollars for a palm reading and fifteen for a look into Madame Cherise's crystal ball. It was situated right next to the baseball game. I briefly wondered if Raine knew Madame Cherise. I knew there was somewhat of a network where psychics could exchange ideas and set prices for certain skills. Even though she owned one, Raine had always poo-pooed the crystal ball as a 'charlatan's tool', all for show but with no real powers. I myself had always been a stalwart skeptic about things like palm readings and talking to the spirit world, until I'd found myself having regular conversations and arguments with a ghost. My best friend, Raine, had proven hers skills more than once with her uncanny predictions. And, while she'd never conjured or spoken with Edward, even when he was sitting in the same room, she always seemed to sense when he was near. Inexplicably, Jackson seemed to have the same sixth sense when it came to Edward. I wasn't sure why, but

I'd gotten fairly practiced at making excuses for unexplained events.

As we strolled past the fortune teller's tent, the flaps fluttered open, and a man with dark hair, gray sideburns and a thick moustache practically stumbled out of the tent wearing a broad, satisfied smile. The scent of incense followed behind him. He was in a blue t-shirt but his cap matched the teal and pink stripes on the tents.

The man's smile was still stuck on his face as he squinted and pointed at Jackson. "Detective Jackson, right?" He walked right toward us with hand outstretched. As he neared, the scent of a woman's perfume mingled with the smell of incense lingering on his shirt.

Jackson stuck out his hand. "Yes, Mr. Stockton, good to see you."

"Please, call me, Carson. And be sure to thank Chief Walker for sending extra patrols around at night. They'll be a big help for keeping troublemakers from hanging around the place after the carnival closes down for the evening."

"That's good to hear. I'll let him know." Jackson looked at me. "Carson, this is my girlfriend, Sunni Taylor. She's a journalist for the *Junction Times*. Sunni, Carson Stockton is the owner of the carnival."

Carson chuckled. "I suppose if you're a reporter, you've already figured that out since it's called the Stockton Traveling Carnival."

"I wondered if it was just coincidence." I shook his hand and glanced behind him at the psychic's tent. "Good news or bad?" I asked.

Both men looked at me in confusion.

"Your fortune?" I added. "We noticed you were coming out of Madame Cherise's tent."

"Oh, right." A dark pink blush covered his neck and headed toward his face. "Yes, well, that was just carnival business." He placed a friendly hand against Jackson's arm. "You'll have to stop by the cotton candy kiosk. Ivonne will want to say hello."

Jackson laughed. "You've got her making cotton candy, eh?"

Carson's thick brow arched, and he leaned closer. "She's not happy about it either, but the usual girl is on maternity leave. Not many people know how to make the cotton candy correctly. It's a lost art—as they say." He glanced at his watch. "I've got to get over to the stage. They'll be announcing the name of the carnival queen soon, and I need to make sure the decorations are ready. Nice seeing you."

He hurried off toward a portable stage that was being decked out with gold balloons and silver paper stars.

"I take it Ivonne is Carson's wife?" I asked.

"Yes, they've been running the carnival together for twenty years. They got married young. Carson inherited it from his dad." Something had caught Jackson's attention over my shoulder. "Raine's walking this way with one of those deep fried cupcakes on a stick."

I spun around. Sure enough, Raine was sweeping through the crowd in one of her long, colorful skirts and a pink and yellow head scarf. Her bangles glistened in the sunlight as she lifted the fried cupcake to her mouth and took a bite.

She headed straight toward us. "Who knew you could deep fry a cupcake. It sort of tastes like an extreme donut. Not that I've ever had or even know what an extreme donut is, but I think this would qualify." She scrunched her nose. "I'm sure I'm going to regret this later." She lowered her lump of fried dough. "Didn't think I'd see you here, what with this morning's incident and all. Poor Lana. I warned her she might fall and hurt herself."

My eyes widened. "You predicted her fall off the stepladder?"

"Huh? No. I'm just always telling her to watch out. She spends so much time on ladders—it doesn't take a psychic to predict a high possibility of falling. Guess we're both going to have to pitch in for the party next weekend. Hey, Jax." Raine finally took a moment to actually greet us. She tended to do the same thing on the phone—just spin past the hello and right into whatever was on her mind. And with Raine, that could be a wide range of topics. She elbowed Jackson and winked. "Are you two heading over to the Lovers' Lane ride? It's as corny as ever. I went on it alone," she said without one ounce of self-pity. The opposite, in fact. Raine had told me more than once that she just didn't have the patience or attention span for a boyfriend.

Jackson grinned down at me. "Forgot all about the Lovers' Lane ride."

"I'm sure it's as romantic as a trip to the grocery store. Where are you heading?" I asked Raine.

She pointed back over her shoulder. "I'm here to see my friend, Cherise Duvay. Actually, we're just casual acquaintances, but I always make a point of dropping in on her crystal ball world." Raine mimed a crystal ball reader by dragging her hand around an invisible sphere. She ended the act with an eye roll. "Cherise is not exactly what one would call a top of the line psychic," she said in a low voice.

Jackson started to laugh but quickly and wisely stifled it.

"I wondered if you two might know each other. I know how you like to network with other psychics," I said. "We won't keep you. There was mention of cotton candy earlier and after standing here, staring at your lump of fried dough, my taste buds are craving sugar."

"I'll see you later at Lana's. She mentioned something about filling goodie bags." Raine waved her stick of cupcake and swished away toward Madame Cherise's tent.

Jackson and I followed the distinct fragrance of fluffy sugar to the cotton candy booth.

"Sometimes I wonder how you and Raine became such close friends. The two of you have nothing in common," Jackson noted.

I smiled up at him. "Exactly. Why would I want to hang out with someone like me? Raine is colorful and fun. Life's never dull around her."

Jackson put his arm around my shoulders and pulled me against his side. "Interesting. Those are the exact reasons I like to hang around you."

"Oh really? Are those the only reasons?" I asked, peering up at him with a bat of my eyelashes.

"There are some other nice perks, but you get the gist." He lowered his arm and fished his wallet from his pocket. "Do you want pink or blue cotton candy? Because I'll be happy to kiss those lips wearing either color."

"Well then, blue it is," I said.

A woman with thick auburn hair tucked under a hairnet was leaned over a large metal vat circling a white paper cone around the perimeter. Gossamer strands of runaway cotton candy clung to her white apron, her arms and even her chin. Her face was pink and beads of perspiration dotted her forehead. She had lovely green eyes, which lit up like stars when she spotted Jackson looming over the cotton candy stand.

"Detective Jackson," she chirruped and then swiped at a strand of cotton candy that flew past her face. She held up a half-covered paper cone. "As you see, I've been saddled with the cotton candy booth for the day." She afforded me a half-smile. I nodded my hello, deciding that was the most a half smile deserved. She stopped the machine for a moment and wiped her hands on a wet cloth. Feathery strings of sugar floated through the air as if the entire booth defied gravity. The weightless sugar was everywhere. I wondered how long she'd have to stand in the shower just to get rid of the stickiness.

"Ivonne, this is my girlfriend, Sunni," Jackson said.

This time the smile was a little more than half. "Nice to meet you. I'd shake your hand but then we'd be glued together for the

19

rest of the day." She took a step and looked down at her feet. "I might even have to throw away my shoes after this stint." She smiled (a whole one) up at Jackson. "Have you seen Carson yet?"

"Yes, actually we have," Jackson said. "We spotted him coming out of the—" Jackson paused and restarted. "He was heading over to make sure the stage was set for the crowning ceremony."

"Then I guess he forgot all about the paper cones I asked him to bring," Ivonne said somewhat angrily. "That man can't remember anything. Oh well. Did you want some cotton candy?" She grinned. "Made it myself."

"Yes, a blue one please." Jackson pulled the money from his wallet.

Ivonne handed me a blue cotton candy. Jackson paid and said his goodbye. We turned and headed back toward the game area.

"I'm curious," I said over a quick nibble of cotton candy. "What made you hesitate back there? You were about to mention you saw her husband coming out of Cherise's tent, but you stopped and, as my phone would say, rerouted. Did it have anything to do with the perfume smell and satisfied grin Carson Stockton was wearing when he stumbled out of the fortune teller's tent?"

Jackson reached for a pinch of the sugar. "And that's why you are an awesome journalist, Bluebird. You never miss a note."

CHAPTER 4

*I*t quickly dawned on me that the announcement of the Spring Fair Queen was not a surprise or highly antici-pated contest where people waited to hear who had won the coveted rhinestone crown. A statuesque girl, with long brown bangs hanging over almond shaped blue eyes, stood near the stage, being admired and adored by a group of friends. Her makeup looked professionally done, although anyone's makeup looked professional next to my haphazard slashes of mascara and dots of blush, so what did I know.

Carnival goers were starting to fill the metal fold-up chairs that had been set in semi-circles around the stage. A grandly decorated throne, a carpenter's attempt at a regal seat, sat in the center of the stage waiting for its royal bottom.

Jackson and I decided to stand behind the rows of seats to get a glimpse of the ceremony.

He leaned his head so I could hear him over the excited murmur coming from the audience. "Were you ever a home-coming or prom queen?" he asked from the side of his mouth.

I couldn't stifle a laugh. I glanced up at him. "Oh, you were serious with that question. Sorry. Thought you were being facetious. I was more the most valuable player type. Emily was the queen of her prom, of course," I added. "Although, she never really liked the notoriety. But frankly, she was born for the role."

"I wish I'd seen you play ball. I'll bet you were pretty formidable on that pitching mound."

I nodded. "I did notice the occasional batter walking toward the box with a quivering bottom lip. I'll win you that unicorn after this."

Carson Stockton had changed into a dress shirt and teal blue coat and tie, but he was still wearing the same faded jeans we'd seen him in earlier. He spoke into the microphone a few times before sound blurted out, along with an ear piercing whistle.

Everyone's shoulders rose up in reaction to the annoying sound.

"Why do microphones do that?" I asked wiggling my finger in my ear. "Is it some kind of requirement in the microphone rules of engagement handbook?"

Jackson laughed. "No, I think it's just really old equipment and a squirt of feedback."

I leaned my head so it rested against his arm. "I've deduced that the queen already knows she's got this thing in the bag. I see a very confident, young woman with the haughty air of nobility standing off to the side of the stage."

"Not exactly sure how they pick the queen, but yes, that girl does seem to know the crown is already hers."

Just then, a tall, dark haired man wearing a neon pink shirt emblazoned with Wright Electric joined the group of girls. The future queen's face lit up, and she threw her arms around him.

"Looks like Prince Charming just arrived in the traditional neon pink t-shirt," I noted.

"That's not Prince Charming, but his family does have a nice stash of money. They own Wright Electric, a very successful company. The future queen must be his girlfriend. The founder of the company, Sutton senior, died about five years ago, an accidental electrocution on the job. There was a big story about it going around town. Apparently, Sutton senior always wore a lucky hat on the job, and the day he died, he couldn't find it."

I peered up at Jackson. "They think he died because he couldn't find his lucky hat?"

Jackson gave a half shrug. "That's what people were saying. I heard Junior is very superstitious and goes through an entire ritual every morning before he heads out on a job."

"No kidding. I guess it is a dangerous business, so it's probably better not to tempt fate."

Carson cleared his throat, and the microphone picked up the sound and carried it across the audience. "We'll get started with the ceremony, so please take your seats." The audience quieted down, but the general noise of the carnival continued on around us. A woman near the stage had set up a camera on a tripod. She waved excitedly to the girl waiting for her crown.

"I guess the Queen Mom is going to get the whole coronation on tape," I said.

A few corny speeches followed, then the big moment arrived, and Melinda Bates was crowned Spring Fair Queen. Melinda was thrilled and screaming with joy as if it was the first she'd learned of her win. A red velvet cloak was tied around her shoulders, and a crown of rhinestones was clipped, after some effort by her friends and eventually her mother, to her head. Carson handed her a nice bouquet of pink roses, which she held in her right hand, but it seemed she was more interested that everyone see her left hand, where, even from the distance Jackson and I stood, I spotted a sizeable diamond sparkling on her ring finger.

Carson picked up a bucket filled with metallic confetti and tossed it high into the air above Melinda's head. It stuck to her hair and crown and cape. She looked less than happy about it all. Her mom popped onto stage to help her get some of the pieces free from her hair. After a few minutes of confetti clean-up, Melinda stepped up to the microphone.

"Thank you, everyone," she said a few times into the microphone, which she made sure to grasp with her left hand and its impressive gemstone. "I want to thank the Stocktons and the Spring Fair committee for choosing me for this honor. I'm looking forward to all the events. I'd also like to say thanks to my mom for recording this exciting moment in my life."

She paused and scanned the crowd. Her gaze stopped on the neon pink shirt. "Sutton, please come up here to share this moment with me." The guy in the pink Wright Electric shirt skirted his way around the chairs to the stage.

"Everyone," Queen Melinda continued, with a wide smile plastered across her face. "I have one more announcement that will make this day even more special."

"Gee, I wonder if it has to do with that diamond engagement ring on her finger," I muttered to Jackson.

"What ring?" he asked.

I rolled my eyes. "You're such a man."

"Guilty as charged," he muttered back.

Sutton Wright reached the stage with hands shoved shyly in his pockets. His face was nearly as pink as his shirt as he sidled up next to Melinda.

"Friends, family, subjects," she said with a giggle. "I'd like to announce that Sutton Wright and I are engaged to be married."

The audience cheered and clapped.

"I think I've seen enough of the ceremony," Jackson said. "What do you say we take a ride on the Ferris wheel?"

I gazed up at the dangling buckets. They stuttered along with slow, jerky movements, occasionally getting stuck before moving forward. "I think I'd like to keep my feet on the ground."

"Guess I won't kiss you then," he quipped.

"Ah, there's nothing like a man who is full of humility." I took his hand and we walked along. "Although, I will admit, your kisses do sometimes make me feel as if I'm walking on the moon."

CHAPTER 5

I'd boasted enough about my pitching skills that by the time the young guy running the game booth handed me the baseball, I had lost all confidence. My pitching arm was a good deal older and more out of shape than it had been in high school.

Jackson crossed his arms, waiting for me to throw the greasy, small ball at the tower of very heavy looking milk bottles on the back wall of the booth.

"Now, remember, the last time I played ball, I was still wearing a retainer and the occasional splash of zit cream. Not to mention, we girls throw the ball underhand, something that is not possible at this angle," I said in an effort to lower his expectations.

His gaze drifted to the top of the pyramid of unicorns. "I've already picked the one I want. It has a rainbow horn and blue bow, and I'm naming him Rocco. And, as I recall, you have a dog named Newman who keeps you in good practice."

"Right. Stupid Newman, you blew my cover," I muttered. I positioned my feet and shuffled them back a few times like I used to do for luck on the pitcher's mound. I peered up at the unicorn with the blue bow. "This one's for you, Rocco." I pulled my arm back and fired the ball at the set of bottles. They splattered in every direction. The last one on the bottom corner rocked side to side for a brief second and then fell over like a reluctant tree being cut in the forest.

"Woo hoo!" I cheered. "I've still got it." I threw my arms up and quickly rubbed my right shoulder. "Ouch. I don't remember that pain when I was eighteen."

Jackson pointed Rocco out to the kid, who looked rather stunned at my throw. "Wow, she's pretty good for her age," he said as he handed Jackson the toy.

Jackson took my hand and spun me away from the game booth before I could respond to the kid's comment.

"My age," I grumbled. "I'd like to see that kid knock those bottles down with one throw."

"I have to say, that was pretty darn impressive, Bluebird." Jackson handed me the unicorn. "Now, hold Rocco. I see one of the uniformed officers who was assigned carnival security detail. I'm going to get an update on any problems and see if he needs anything."

"Don't you want to take your new friend along for an introduction?" I held up the unicorn to let him know I was talking about Rocco and not myself.

"Not sure if I could live it down at the precinct. I'll be right back."

I strolled down the middle aisle of game booths, with no particular purpose or destination. I stopped near the fortune teller's tent. Seeing it reminded me of Raine, which reminded me that Lana was going to need my help tonight. The carnival was getting more crowded and somewhat overrun with teenagers. I had a farm and a sister to look after, so it was probably best to cut the day short.

I pulled out my phone to text Lana when two women swooshed past me so fast, I nearly dropped it. The women, one who was possibly in her early twenties and another in her mid to late forties, were wearing matching neon pink t-shirts, the same Wright Electric shirts as Queen Melinda's fiancé, Sutton Wright. The younger woman's hair and skin tone was similar to Sutton's, and it was easy to deduce they were brother and sister, or, at the very least, related. They were so deep in a tense conversation, they hadn't noticed that they nearly smacked into me. They wore serious expressions as they went into Madame Cherise's tent. It seemed they were in urgent need of a fortune telling.

I sent a text to Lana. "I'm at the carnival with Jackson, but we'll be leaving soon. I'll bring you some dinner after I check on the farm."

She rang me back. "Had to call," she said. "Too hard to text with one hand."

"Oh wow, I hadn't thought of that. How are you feeling?"

"My whole arm hurts but I'll live. I called to let you know that Raine is bringing me a submarine sandwich, so I won't need dinner. But if you want to come help fill party favor bags, I wouldn't say no."

"Sure, I can do that." Jackson's tall, dark head towered over most everyone else as he lumbered back toward me. "I've got to stop by the farm first."

There was a ruckus behind me. I looked back over my shoulder. The queen and her apparent entourage were making their rounds, handing out stickers and free balloons to kids. I stepped out of their way. Melinda stopped to show a few women her ring, and the oohs and ahhs followed.

"Jeez, I'm sorry about that, Sunni. I should be helping you with the farm," Lana said.

"Not a big deal, although Emi stuck King Harold in with the hens and . . . well . . . there was a short, fierce battle with an empty feed bucket. I lost, by the way."

Lana snickered. "Oops, sorry, I shouldn't laugh. It's the pain killer. I've faced down that beast a few times, and he is scary. Take a broom in next time. The bucket allows him to get too close. And as Nick once told me, King Harold can smell fear a mile away, so act casual as if you couldn't care less about him."

Jackson reached me and waited while I finished my call.

"All brave words from a woman sitting on her couch, loopy on pain pills and waiting for her dinner to be delivered. But thanks, I will try the broom trick. Hey, I've got to go. I'll see you in a few hours."

"I'll be here," she sighed.

Jackson took hold of Rocco and pushed him under one arm while dropping his free arm around my shoulder. "Was that Lana?" he asked.

"Yes. She advised me to take a broom into the chicken yard, so I have a fighting chance against King Harold."

He nodded. "Sounds like solid advice. How is she feeling?"

"She sounded a little depressed, but Raine is bringing her a sandwich. I'm going over there later to help with some party favors. Did the officer have any problems to report?" I asked as we headed through the maze of people.

"No problems. Looks like it's going to be a trouble-free week at the carnival."

CHAPTER 6

*J*ackson was kind enough to help with dinner hour at the farm. The chickens were in for the night, and it really only required a double check on Emily's horse, Butterscotch, and my two favorite barn critters, the goats, Cuddlebug and Tinkerbell.

After a nice, long kiss goodbye, Jackson headed home, and I climbed into my jeep for the short drive to Lana's house. Raine's car was sitting out front as I pulled up.An unfamiliar red bicycle, complete with basket and colorful handlebar tassels, was leaned against the side of the house. Raine's voice rolled toward me as I opened the front door. It was accompanied by another voice I didn't recognize.

Lana was sitting at her kitchen table, looking less than excited about entertaining guests. She had regained most of the color in her face, but the lines on her forehead showed she was still in pain.

Raine noticed me first. She pushed her glasses higher on her nose and smiled. "There you are, Sunni. I thought I might have to fill all those bags myself." She motioned toward Lana's long maple table where girlie goodies like shiny tubs of lip gloss, beaded bracelets and hairclips were heaped in piles.

"I had to check the farm," I reminded her.

I smiled politely at the other woman. She was wearing a gold leather jacket. Leopard print short boots peered out from her black bellbottoms. A bright blue headband crossed her forehead and disappeared under a curly mound of blonde hair.

"Oh," Raine chirped, "I forgot to introduce you two. Sunni, this is Cherise Duvay. She works for the Stockton Carnival. Cherise, this is Lana's sister and my best friend, Sunni Taylor. She owns the big brick mansion you rode past on your way to Lana's."

Cherise's headband perked up at the mention of my *mansion*, a term that couldn't be farther from the truth in its current state. "You live in the Cider Ridge Inn? I've heard that place is literally bursting with ghosts." She turned back to Raine. "Why on earth didn't you tell me your best friend owned the place?" She picked up her cup of soda and drew a long noisy sip. "Have you connected with any of the lost souls yet?" To my relief, she directed her question to Raine.

Raine shrugged nonchalantly. "Haven't had much time to focus on it." Apparently, she was going avoid the mention of her failed séance. "Sunni is having the entire house restored so it can be used as a bed and breakfast." Raine emptied the last few potato chips from the bag onto her plate.

Cherise's gold coat reflected the light from the overhead pendants as she sat forward with interest. "Oh boy, you know that's never a good idea—" She continued even though none of us prodded her to elaborate. She lowered her voice to a conspiratorial lull as she spoke across the table to Raine. "You know how freaked out regular people get when unhappy spirits are lingering about."

Raine was drawn right into the conversation, almost as if Lana and I, (regular people, I presumed) weren't standing right in the room with her. "Yes, I think it could be a bonus for marketing though. Don't you think? There are plenty of people who would find it exciting to stay in a haunted inn. You know, people without a finely honed sixth sense," she said demurely, almost like a rich woman taking pity on people who don't have a live-in chef. It was one of those many moments when I badly wanted to blurt that just this morning my unhappy spirit was lecturing me about staying out too late.

I glanced discretely toward Lana, who looked as if she badly wanted to go to bed. She'd hardly touched the sandwich on her plate. I pulled up a chair at the table.

"Would you like half of my sandwich?" Lana asked. "I don't have much appetite."

Raine looked at me with the same expression my mom used to wear when she was telling me that I was making bad decisions. "I told her she needs to fill her stomach if she's taking pain medicine, otherwise that stuff will go straight to her head."

"Isn't that the point of them?" Lana asked wryly.

"It's true about eating first," Cherise added with the same motherly confidence as Raine. "Those chemicals will burn right through the lining of the stomach if it's not coated with food." Apparently, a finely honed sixth sense also gave you vast medical expertise.

Lana was anxious to get off the topic of her pain. "How was the carnival, Sunni?"

"Oh, were you at the carnival?" Cherise asked before I had a chance to respond. I was tempted to look disappointed and ask her why she didn't already sense that I'd been there, but I didn't want Raine to be upset with me. She was acting a little oddly in the presence of another psychic, and I found it kind of cute. (I would never tell her that, of course.)

"Yes, I was there with my boyfriend." If Cherise hadn't been sitting at the table, I would have leapt into a diatribe about how shabby and out of date the carnival was and how badly it needed to be refurbished. Instead, I listed our activities. "We ate some cotton candy, or, I should say, I ate some cotton candy. Jackson was going to try a deep fried cupcake but then he saw Raine swinging hers around like a heavy piece of dough and decided his stomach was against the whole thing. I made up for it by winning him a fuzzy, stuffed unicorn with a blue bow and rainbow colored horn." I circled my shoulder around once. "I've still got a golden arm." I grinned smugly at Lana. Lana had been the busy over-achiever in high school, head of every club and editor for the year-book. She considered sports a waste of time. "We also watched the crowning of the Spring Fair Queen. And the highlight of that moment came when Queen Melinda announced to the crowd that she is engaged to Sutton Wright. His family owns an—"

"An electric company," Lana finished. "They're the biggest in the area."

Cherise was picking at the crust on her roll as she clucked her tongue, hoping to get our attention.

Raine looked at her. "What's up? Do you know something about the engagement?"

Cherise shrugged her gold covered shoulders. "Let's just say, I don't think that engagement will last." We waited for a few more details, but she was sticking to her 'let's just say' plan.

"Do you know the Wrights?" I asked, recalling the two women in the pink t-shirts nearly plowing into me in their hurry to get to Madame Cherise's tent.

"Me?" she said, with some surprise. "I don't know them. It's just something I heard." She waved her long blue nails to end the conversation. "Well, it's been wonderful talking to all of you, but I need to ride back to the carnival. It's getting late. Thank you for having me," she said to Lana. "And coat that stomach lining." She turned to me. "Maybe you have time this week to give me a quick tour of your old house. I'd love to make a few contacts with the Cider Ridge spirits."

33

"Spirit," Raine said sharply. It seemed Cherise had finally stepped on a nerve. Raine considered the Cider Ridge ghost her own personal haunting. "It's one spirit, a male, Edward Beckett, who died in a duel over his true love."

I snickered once, but stifled it quickly. I'd learned long ago that the romanticized version of the duel for Bonnie had been embellished through the years. After hearing Edward's version of the story, it was more of a pride thing. In those days, when one was challenged to a duel, a man had no choice but to accept. Otherwise, he'd be branded a coward. Edward had been a scoundrel, of that I was certain, but, apparently, he was no coward.

Raine walked Cherise to the front door.

"Lana, go to bed. Raine and I will get these party favor bags filled. Then you'll have one less thing to worry about."

Lana agreed reluctantly with a weak head nod. "I think I *will* go to bed, if you two can handle it."

I quirked a brow at her. "One item of each in a bag? I think we can manage not to screw it up."

"You're right. Sorry, not myself. As you can tell." Lana picked up her plate with her left hand. "I guess I'll wrap this sandwich for tomorrow."

I got up and took the plate from her. "Believe it or not, my college degree actually qualifies me for sandwich wrapping, as well. Now, off with you. Do you need help getting dressed or brushing teeth?"

"I can manage." She shuffled toward the stairs. I'd never, ever seen my sister Lana shuffle. She was definitely out of it.

"Maybe I should stay the night," I called to her.

"Nope, I'll be fine. Just lock up when you leave."

Raine returned to the kitchen. "Did Lana go to bed?" We sat down at the work table, behind the mounds of teenage treats.

"Yes, I insisted, and she put up no argument. Do you think she'll be all right here alone tonight?" I asked.

"I think she'll probably just sleep through the night. Besides, you're not far away if she needs you. I could stay, but I've got an eight o-clock Tarot card reading."

"No, you're right. I'm close by if she needs me." I sighed at the monotonous task in front of us. "How about you fill the bag up to the henna tattoo stickers, and I'll take it from the Hello Kitty key chains."

"Sounds like a plan." Raine picked up the first cellophane bag. 'Carli's Sweet Sixteen' was printed in lavender across the plastic. "That Cherise is such a character. And whatever you do, don't give her a tour of the inn. She'll probably just make up some story about talking to a ghost just for publicity."

I briefly wondered if Raine was worried that Cherise would have more luck conjuring a ghost than her. "Not a problem. I had no intention of inviting her. How long has she been traveling with the carnival?"

"Far as I know, since she was nineteen. She started in some of the grunt jobs, clean up, filling soda cups, that kind of stuff. Then she declared herself a psychic and talked the owners into letting her set up a fortune telling tent. Just between you and me—" she leaned in. My best friend was in a particularly catty mood this evening. "I think she's having an affair with a married man." She dropped a tube of cherry lip gloss into the bag.

The sight of the carnival owner stumbling out of Cherise's tent with a satisfied grin popped into my head. "Oh really?" I asked. "What makes you think that?"

"She was anxious to catch me up on her social life. Most likely because her psychic life was as flat as her talents." She suppressed an amused grin. "She told me she had a new boyfriend and that she hoped, if things worked out, they could one day be together permanently. She also wouldn't tell me a thing about him." She dropped a roll of root beer flavored candies into the bag. "What else could that mean, except she's dating a married man."

"Unless he's some secret agent for the government," I said.

Raine laughed off my suggestion. "Please, Cherise is far too airheaded for that."

"Boy, you really don't think much of her, do you?" I took the bag from her and started dropping in my half of the goodies.

"She's nice enough, I suppose." Raine sounded a bit contrite about saying so many negative things about Cherise. "It's just that she's the kind of psychic—and I'd hold up air quotes if I wasn't holding a bag of goodies—that gives those of us who take the profession seriously, a bad name."

"Ah, I see. That makes sense. There are journalists—and excuse my lack of air quotes too—" I held up the bag I was filling. "That give journalists a bad name. In fact, I work with one. Chase has almost no interest in writing or journalism or reporting. Apparently, he just stays at the paper because he has a sweet deal being engaged to the newspaper owner's daughter."

"See, so you know exactly how I feel. Chase gets all the gritty stories, but you're the true writer. By the way, what are you working on right now?"

"I find out my new assignment tomorrow. With my luck, it'll be something dull and trivial, like covering the Spring Fair Carnival." I put the finished bag at the end of the table and looked back at the piles of goodies. "Jeez, this is going to take longer than I thought. I think I'll put on a kettle for tea."

CHAPTER 7

t was only nine o'clock on Monday morning, yet it felt as if I'd already lived through an entire week. I had hurried through my usual morning at home, making sure the dogs had everything they needed, checking that Ursula and Henry were set for the day and that Edward was resolved to stay upstairs and out of the way of any of the live human action downstairs. I nibbled buttered toast as I rushed out the door, jumped into the jeep and raced to Lana's to make sure she had everything she needed. She was groggy but feeling better, well enough to accept the scrambled eggs breakfast I'd offered to cook. Then I nibbled a second piece of buttered toast, this one with a splotch of marmalade, as I raced back to the jeep and jumped inside for the short trip to Emily's farm. It took a good hour to get everyone fed and watered and the eggs collected before I once again, this time without the toast, raced to my jeep for the considerably longer drive to the newspaper office.

Myrna, the irreplaceable office manager, motioned her head silently toward the editor's office door. She was trying out a bright pink lipstick shade that was a good deal easier on the eyes than the neon orange she wore last week. Myrna changed lipstick color as often as I changed socks. She loved makeup and experimented with bold color choices. It took a while to get used to. It was all part of her fun personality. But today, her expression wasn't saying 'fun'. Her eyes flicked the direction of Parker Seymour's door with a good dose of trepidation.

I raised my shoulders and held out my arms to mimic a hulking, angry bear and motioned my own head toward Parker's door.

A dark curl fell on her forehead as she nodded emphatically. It seemed my boss's mood had necessitated a silent conversation between us. Myrna was rarely wordless. This didn't bode well for my tardiness or my next assignment. I walked to my desk and noticed that Chase's chair was empty, and his usual cup of coffee was nowhere to be seen. I cleared my throat to get Myrna's attention.

She looked up from her computer. I pointed to Chase's desk and then to the editor's door, trying to ascertain if the *lead reporter* was inside with the boss. Myrna's response was a head shake that sent her dangling bead earrings into a shimmery dance.

I lifted my hands at my shoulders to let her know I didn't understand what was going on. "O.K. this is silly, Myrna. I've already had an epically long morning, what's up?" I said it in a hushed tone, still not wanting to alert the bear and lure him from his cave.

Myrna got up from her desk, which was much closer to Parker's office than my lone island at the far end of the room. She floated across the floor on her dancer's feet and leaned down. "He's in an absolutely terrible mood. He's taking grumpy to a whole new level this morning."

I winced as if she'd just inflicted pain. "Is it because I'm late?"

"No," she paused, "although that is probably not going to help *you* this morning. Why are you so late?"

I sighed and shook my head. "Because I'm taking care of the

entire family, animals included, for the next few days." We both spoke in hushed tones as if we were inside a library with a particularly volatile librarian. "What has him in such a lather? Another possible case of the flu?" My perfectly robust boss was so afraid of germs, he washed his hands hourly and worried that every sneeze meant impending doom. I was sure it was a difficult way to live, and there were times when I felt bad for him. But at the same time, it made working for him much harder.

We were talking so softly we had to lean closer to each other. "Now that Chase and Rebecca are engaged, Parker thinks his days as editor are numbered," Myrna whispered. "He's certain that Newsom will move his son-in-law up to the editor position to keep the paper in the family—so to speak."

I glanced back at Chase's empty chair. "Where is our star reporter? Already hard at work on a riveting story?" It was hard to speak in hushed tones when the words were dripping in sarcasm.

"No, he and Rebecca are out looking at new houses. Daddy Newsom is going to put a large down payment on a house for a wedding gift," Myrna said with an eye roll.

"Well, I don't think I could ever work under Chase Evans, so let's hope nepotism doesn't rear its ugly head in this newspaper office."

"I better head back to my desk before *he* bursts out of his office." Mryna did a beautiful little pirouette halfway back to her desk. She'd taken up dancing as a hobby at my suggestion, and she was enjoying it immensely.

She was just settling behind her desk when Parker's door flew open. Myrna and I shot each other a wide-eyed look.

"Taylor," Parker barked, "why are you late?" He was carrying one of his famous manila folders. I could only assume it held the details (which were usually few and far between) for my next assignment.

I straightened my posture to let him know his gruffness was

not going to intimidate me, even though there was a slight tremor in my hands. "My sister injured herself yesterday. She broke her wrist, and I stopped at her house to check on her and make her breakfast. She's still in a great deal of pain." I felt a tad guilty using my sister's bad luck as a way out of trouble, but the whole excuse was true. It wasn't as if I was giving some outlandish tall tale about the dog eating my homework or having to lecture my house ghost about not disturbing the construction crew. Although, occasionally I'd been tempted to throw the latter out there just to see how people reacted.

Parker pulled his lips in, seemingly not expecting my perfectly decent excuse for being tardy. "Oh well, that's a shame," he said with a low grumble. "Give her my best."

Once again, I was feeling a touch sorry for the man. He probably had every right to be worried about his position. Chase's relationship with the newspaper owner's daughter had kept him in the entirely undeserved position of lead reporter. It seemed quite possible that he could move right up into another unearned and undeserved position like editor.

"Thank you, Parker, I will. Would you like to meet right now about my next assignment?" I asked.

"No need for a meeting." He dropped the folder on my desk. "There's a carnival in town. I'd like you to write up an article about it. The entire enterprise is a shabby, outdated mess, but the owner, Carson Stockton, is a friend of the mayor's so make it glowing." With that he turned on his loafers and headed straight back to his office. His door snapped smartly shut.

Myrna gave me the 'told you so' head nod. I picked up the folder and opened it. There were just three words typed across an otherwise blank sheet of paper, *Stockton Traveling Carnival*. Ugh.

CHAPTER 8

*P*arker usually gave me a few phone numbers and contacts to give me a start on a story, but since he was too steeped in his own miserable mood to provide me anything except the obvious name of the carnival along with the reminder to make it glowing, I made a few calls and finally connected with Carson Stockton. He was jovial enough on the phone, and when I told him my name, he knew right away that Detective Jackson had introduced us the day before. He was more than happy to sit for an interview.

I'd given myself a pep talk all the way to the carnival parking lot. There would be better stories in my future, and when the Cider Ridge Inn was finished, I'd be able to leave the newspaper and start my new career as innkeeper. Then I would be my own boss, and I would no longer have to deal with grumpy editors.

A gloomy clump of clouds, ripe with spring showers, hung low over the faded tents and awnings as I walked up to the carnival gates. A man wearing a puffy green parka and teal and pink striped cap was sitting at the gate with a clipboard and a self-important posture.

"We're not open to the public for another hour," he said, long before I reached the gate.

I pulled my press pass out of my coat pocket. "I'm here from the *Junction Times*. I have an appointment with Carson Stockton. The name is Sunni Taylor."

His dark brow furrowed with more skepticism. It was obvious he took his job quite seriously. He ran his finger down the paper on the clipboard. "Oh yeah, Carson just added you to the list." He reached into his puffy coat pocket and pulled out a heavy ring of keys. He unlocked the padlock and slid open the chain link gate just enough for me to slip through.

I thanked the man with a smile. "If it's not too much trouble, could you point me in Mr. Stockton's direction?"

"Sure thing." He was much friendlier now that I was a listed guest. "If you walk past the hamburger and shake stand and make a quick left you'll see a line of RVs. Carson's is the first one on the row."

"Thanks again." Carnival employees, or carnies as they were historically called, were getting their game and food booths ready for the crowds. The young man who had been stunned by the *old woman's* pitching arm at the baseball throw game was stuck with the monotonous task of filling pink and teal balloons with helium. Each balloon had the name Stockton Carnival printed across its girth. The long row of helium tanks leaned up against the pizza stand indicated a lengthy morning of balloon filling for the guy. Considering his comment about my age, I silently reveled in that notion.

The Ferris wheel chortled to life and began to spin. A tall, well built man wearing a green striped shirt, tool belt and enough grease in his hair to take the squeak out of the Ferris wheel was standing at the control panel for the ride, apparently checking all its 'bells and whistles' or whatever it was a ride mechanic might check on a Ferris wheel.

I continued on toward the hamburger stand where the smoky char of coals was already filling the air with the promise of grilled burgers. Six long motorhomes were parked a good distance back from the carnival in the RV park.

I wasn't completely sure what I would ask the carnival owner, but I hoped something would come to me. I was just a few feet from the portable metal steps leading up to the motorhome when the door swung violently open. Carson's wife, Ivonne, pounded angrily down the steps on heavy feet. Her face was red with rage. She was so caught up in emotion, she swept right past me without a word.

I paused, wondering if I was just about to catch Carson at the wrong time. But then my reporter's feet moved quickly toward the steps. Maybe this wouldn't be such a dull assignment after all. Parker told me to write a glowing review of the carnival itself, but he never mentioned I had to gloss over details about the people running it. After Carson's blissful stumble out of Madame Cherise's tent, the day before, I wondered if there was an entire soap opera going on behind the scenes. It made sense, considering that during carnival season, the people working for the Stocktons traveled from town to town with their own little nomadic family. Members of a traveling carnival had to spend a lot of time with their coworkers.

I walked lightly up the steps and peered through the small window in the top of the door. Two large desks sat on each side of the space in front a small kitchenette, complete with built in table and bench. At the rear of the interior, a small ladder led up to a loft with beds.

Carson was bent over, his elbows resting on the desk and his head in his hands. I knocked lightly on the door that Ivonne Stockton had left unlatched. It fell open. It took Carson a second to lift his head. His face was nearly as red as his wife's, but he looked far more distraught than angry.

His forehead bunched in deep lines. "Yes, can I help you?" His mood had certainly darkened since our phone call.

I walked with tender footsteps farther into the trailer. The forehead lines smoothed.

"Oh, yes, Miss Taylor. I'm sorry. I forgot you were coming." He fiddled with a few papers on his desk, and as his big hands moved, he accidentally knocked over a cup of coffee. Brown liquid ran in thin rivers toward his paperwork. He grabbed up the papers and muttered a string of curse words under his breath.

"Can I get you some paper towels from one of the food stands?" I offered.

He didn't answer but grabbed several sheets of clean paper from his printer and tossed them over the spill to soak up the coffee. "I'm sorry but it seems you've caught me at a bad time. Maybe you could interview a few of the workers. Calvin Hooper, our maintenance man, is on the grounds right now checking all the rides. You could shadow him and find out how we keep the rides working safely. People like to hear about that kind of stuff."

"Yes, I suppose ride safety is always of interest. If you're sure you don't have time right now for an interview."

He stood up. "No, I don't. I need to make a few calls, so if you don't mind—" He walked toward the door to assure me that we were through. "I'm sure Calvin won't mind showing you around. Just let him know I sent you and that he should make sure you get the safety checklist." We were at the door by the time he finished. He forced a smile. "Calvin is wearing a green striped shirt and a tool belt. I see the Ferris wheel is moving. That's where you'll find him." The man was so anxious to be rid of me, I half expected him to give me a nudge out the door.

"Right. I'll head over to the Ferris wheel then. Thank you and I'm sorry I caught you at such a bad time." I waited, hoping he'd fill in a few details about his morning, but he responded by shutting the door.

I headed toward the Ferris wheel. It stopped spinning before I passed the hamburger stand, so I picked up my pace. I was just reaching the corner that, once turned, would take me to the Ferris wheel control station when angry words stopped my progress. I backed up to hide behind a large cutout of an ice cream cone and peered around the vanilla swirl to eavesdrop.

Cherise, the fortune teller, was standing with her hands on the hips of her blue leather pants as she chewed out Calvin, the maintenance man. I couldn't see her face, but it was obvious from the rigid posture that she was mad. Calvin looked fairly cool and collected, considering she was waving a long blue fingernail in his face as she finished her scolding.

"And I told you to stay out of my business," Cherise snapped. "You keep to your side of the carnival and I'll keep to mine."

Calvin reached into his tool belt and pulled out a rather menacing looking screwdriver. I gasped, worried that he might have more nefarious reasons for pulling out the tool than a minor adjustment on the control panel. Cherise, however, wasn't worried or deterred in the slightest. She pushed her face close to his. "Don't let me find you snooping around my tent anymore."

Calvin gripped the screwdriver in his hand. I was just about to jump into action, to make myself visible, when Calvin turned around and faced the control panel. He turned his back on Cherise and jammed the tip of the screwdriver into the corner screw of the panel. I released the breath I'd been holding.

Voices from behind startled me. I grabbed the cardboard display to keep it from falling over. Two young women, both with pink and teal t-shirts, walked past. They stared at the strange woman behind the ice cream and rightly so. I smiled weakly and waved.

"I just love soft serve ice cream, don't you?" I said.

They kept walking without offering their opinion on the matter. I stayed tucked behind the ice cream as Cherise swept past in a cloud of perfume. She was in her own angry muddle and didn't notice me.

Once she was around the corner, I stepped out from behind the cardboard cutout. Calvin was busy leaned over the control panel, working with the lethal looking screwdriver to get the metal cover off. I cleared my throat.

"I'm through listening to you, Cherise. Go find someone else to screech at," he said.

I cleared my throat again, and he peeled his focus away from his task. "Actually, I'm from the *Junction Times*." I lifted my press pass from my pocket. "I'm doing a write up about the carnival for the local paper. Carson suggested I shadow you for the morning to watch you perform the safety check on the rides."

He puffed out a loud burst of air and shook his head. "This morning just keeps getting better."

"If I'm in the way, maybe I could find someone else to interview." I was already not looking forward to shadowing a maintenance man on his safety check. Now, it seemed, I was going to be shadowing a grumpy man. There sure seemed to be a lot of them around the carnival this morning, and it seemed all of their sour moods were somehow connected to the fortune teller.

CHAPTER 9

*A*fter one of the longest hours of my life, following the less than congenial Calvin, the maintenance man, around the maze of carnival rides and gaining absolutely nothing from the tour, except the solid decision not to step foot on any of the attractions, I found myself wandering through the early carnival crowd. It seemed the morning hours were more attractive to the families with young children, which made sense considering how early little ones got up from bed when on vacation. My mom used to complain that it took a human-sized can opener to pry us from bed on school mornings, but we ejected from bed at the crack of dawn during spring and summer break. Of course, that all changed once we hit the teen years, which would also explain the lack of teenagers attending the carnival this morning.

I strolled past the fortune telling tent. Cherise had hung a sign that said readings would begin at noon. I'd briefly considered interviewing her, unsure of where to turn to next, but it seemed she was out for the morning. It was just as well. It wasn't as if I could straight up ask her if she was having an affair with the owner. Not that it was beyond me as a journalist. I never shied from tough questions, but I didn't want to upset Raine. It would be too easy for Cherise to piece together where I got my information.

Feeling utterly uninspired, I made the desperate decision to interview some of the workers at the food stands. Maybe the carnies deep frying cupcakes could add a little zip to the story. I headed down the main aisle where food booths were lined up on both sides, offering every morsel from deep fried pickles to jalapeno kettle corn. I perused the stands, not for the most daring food choice but for the carnival employee who looked the most interesting. I was leaning toward the woman at the snow cone booth only because she was wearing a shirt that said 'no flavor combination too crazy. Just ask'.

I pulled out my notebook and looked at the sad, dull notes I'd taken during my hour with Calvin. What a waste of a morning. As I rethought my strategy about an interview with the snow cone lady, a burst of color came around the corner. The Spring Fair Queen, dressed in her regalia of red velvet cloak and rhinestone crown, was holding a massive bouquet of helium balloons. Anxious little kids surrounded her, waiting for a free balloon.

The scene should have been charming, but it lacked any spark of joy, with the exception of the kids running back to their parents with a bouncy balloon in tow. The queen, however, looked as if she was on the verge of tears as she forced a smile and secured the strings to tiny little wrists. Melinda was flanked, on each side, by her friends. They helped her with the task by pulling single balloons free from the giant bouquet. In between, they seemed to console her and pat her on the red velvet shoulder. There was definitely something amiss with the Spring Fair Queen.

I strolled casually along, trying to overhear their conversation between the excited clamor of little kids and the balloons rubbing against each other.

"Well, I think he'll come around," the friend on her right said with confidence. "It's just—what do they call it—cold turkey," she said with equal assurance.

The other friend leaned over to see her counterpart on the right. "Uh, I think you mean cold feet, Cynthia. I just can't believe anyone can change their mind that quickly," she added.

My gaze flew to Melinda's left hand as she finished tying a pink balloon on the wrist of a little girl wearing a tiger striped shirt and go-go boots to match. The beautiful diamond engagement ring was gone. It seemed something had happened between yesterday's engagement announcement and today's balloon disbursement. My mind dashed back to the brief chat with Cherise in Lana's kitchen. She had mentioned, with no qualifiers or details, that she didn't think the engagement would last. It couldn't have just been coincidence. How would a fortune teller in a traveling carnival have a connection with a couple who lived here in Firefly Junction?

Queen Melinda and her entourage moved on. I followed for a bit, trying to grab a few more slices of information, but there was too much activity around them. It didn't matter much anyhow. It wasn't as if I was going to be able to write my carnival story around the breakup of the Spring Fair Queen's engagement.

My phone buzzed. It was a text from Emily. "How are the animals?" She had no idea about Lana. She would, no doubt, be upset that we didn't tell her about it, but at least this way she could still enjoy her romantic getaway with Nick. Her text reminded me that I needed to drive home at lunch to check on the farm and Lana.

"Everyone is still standing on four legs. And two legs too. Even King Harold."

She wrote right back. "Is he giving you trouble?"

"Not anymore. I think we've reached a truce. Especially because I go inside the yard armed with a broom."

"That rotten rooster," Emily texted back.

"Are you two having a nice time?" I wrote. Certainly, their week had to be going better than mine.

"It's wonderful and the place Nick picked is super cozy. How is Lana? I texted her earlier, but she didn't answer."

I froze and stared down at my phone, quickly trying to find a reason that Lana didn't text back, other than the most probable one that she was taking a nap. Lana was not normally a nap taker, so Emily would know something was up.

"She probably just left her phone somewhere, like in the barn. You know how busy she gets when she's working." I hated lying to Emily, but I had no choice.

"I'm sure you're right," Emily texted. "We'll see you soon."

"Have fun." I put my phone back into my pocket and headed toward the snow cone booth.

The cooler morning air and cloud cover seemed to be hurting snow cone sales. The woman running the machine was scrolling through her phone with seemingly nothing to do. I pulled out my notebook. I was at the carnival to get a story, so I was going to have to toss out my best, most leading questions, the kind of deep, meaningful queries that got to the heart of any good news article.

"Good morning, I'm Sunni Taylor from the *Junction Times*." I flashed my press pass. "I'm writing a story about the carnival. I was hoping I could ask you a few questions."

She lowered her phone and looked slightly surprised that I'd come to her for answers.

"Sure, I guess so."

I held my pen against the paper and squinted at her badge. "Well, Carmen, first question. What is the most popular flavor combination at the snow cone stand?"

50

a fter a riveting morning talking to carnival workers about
snow cone flavors and popular game prizes, I headed to
Emily's farm to check on her furry and feathered children. My
plan was to do a quick survey of the farm, then dash over to Lana's
to fix us lunch. Then I'd go back to the carnival to see if I could
catch Carson in a better mood for an interview.

I drove the jeep along the unpaved road leading up to Emily's
farm and was more than shocked to see Lana's car parked in front
of the chicken yard. I hopped out of the jeep and headed toward
the coops. The hens were busy scratching away at the dirt and
grass picking up microscopic edibles.

Lana was leaned into one of the nesting houses with an egg
collecting basket hanging on the injured arm.

"Why are you collecting eggs when you should be at home resting?" I called across the yard.

My voice startled her. She popped up so fast, she hit the back of
her head on the edge of the nest box. She dropped two eggs into
her half full basket and rubbed her head. "You sneak up on people

just like King Harold." I noted, then, that my weapon of choice, the straw broom, was leaning up against the side of the nest boxes.

"Sorry, I should have announced myself," I said. "Although that probably still would have ended with a head bump." I walked through the two gates that led into the chicken yard. I scanned the feathery crowd for a fiery red comb but didn't see the crazy king.

I carefully lifted the basket off of Lana's arm, making extra sure not to even graze the thick wrap, the temporary cast, on her wrist. "I'm fairly certain carrying heavy baskets and collecting eggs was not on the doctor's list of proper care for you broken wrist."

Lana blew out a puff of frustrated air. "I know but I hate being useless, and we were both supposed to take care of the farm together. It's not fair that I left it all for you."

"Really, I don't mind at all." A flash of red behind her made my heart skip a beat. "Don't look now but the cranky king has just spotted us."

Lana grabbed the broom. "Start toward the gate. I'll cover you."

My laughter contained a twinge of hysteria as I raced toward the gate with the basket of eggs and my sister and her broom sweeping up behind. We made it through without incident. King Harold paced in front of the gate with his red crown held high as if he'd just successfully rid the castle yard of intruders.

All the color had returned to Lana's pink complexion, but I sensed that she was in more pain than she let on. "Why don't you head home," I suggested. "I'll just check on the horse and goats, then I'll make us some lunch. I'm starved. I've been hanging around the carnival all morning breathing in the scent of popcorn, hamburgers and funnel cakes."

"I can help you finish up in the barn," Lana insisted, and I knew too well there was no arguing against her. "I spent the morning trying to make paper star garlands for the party, but the stars looked very sad and un-star-like. That's when I decided to come here. I figured it wouldn't take two working hands to collect eggs and fill water buckets."

"All right. Let's finish up." I glanced up at the sky. Other than the occasional lone raindrop, it seemed the clouds were holding. "I was expecting it to rain by now." We walked across the yard to the barn. "I was thinking I'd let Butterscotch out to stretch her legs, but what kind of aunt would I be if I let one of Emily's babies get wet."

I slid open the barn door. The warm scent of animal, straw and hay surrounded us.

"I'm pretty sure a two thousand pound horse can hold her own in a mild rainstorm, but you're probably right. Emily wouldn't be happy." Lana hung the broom on the rack next to the mucking rakes.

"Speaking of Emily," I grabbed a large pinch of hay off a bale for the goats. "Did you text her back? She was worried about you not responding."

"I didn't text her back because I hate lying to Emily. It's like lying to sweet Grandma Edna or to a fluffy white kitten. I'd be overcome with guilt."

"So you chose the true coward's way out and let your sister deal with the guilt." Cuddlebug and Tinkerbell, Emily's goats, were happy to see me. I couldn't stop myself from going into their stall for some hugs. Lana checked in on the horse. After some good, hearty rubs and squeezes, the girls squirmed free of my exuberant hugs and headed to the pile of hay.

I walked out, locked them in and headed to the horse's stall. Lana was brushing Butterscotch's blonde coat with her left hand. "I can't believe how weak my left arm is compared to my right," she said.

"Yeah, I guess it's something you don't notice until you're forced to rely on the weaker arm. Do you want me to finish grooming her?"

Lana shook her head. "No, if I'm going to have to rely on my left arm for six weeks, I better start breaking it in." She winced. "Bad choice of words but you know what I mean."

I stayed on the outside of the stall and watched Lana work. Butterscotch blithely nibbled on a pile of hay, enjoying the snack and groom combo.

"What did you think of Raine's friend, Cherise?" I asked.

"Gosh, I could hardly tell you. I was kind of out of it last night. I mostly remember a gold coat and a woman lecturing me about coating my stomach with food."

I laughed. "Guess you picked up on the more poignant parts of the evening anyhow."

"Why do you ask?"

"No reason really. She's a fortune teller at the traveling carnival, but Raine doesn't seem too impressed with the woman's psychic skills."

Lana chuckled. "You might have noticed but Raine tends to be kind of judgy when it comes to psychic skills."

"Yes, that's true. It's just, Cherise seemed to be right about something she said last night. Yesterday at the fair, the girl who was crowned Spring Fair Queen made the announcement that she was engaged to Sutton Wright. With no details given, Cherise mentioned that she didn't think the engagement would last. And today, it seemed that prediction came true. The queen was shuffling around the carnival looking distraught and short one diamond ring."

"Maybe Cherise has more talent than Raine wants to admit." Lana patted Butterscotch's neck. "That's the best I can do, pretty girl, with my weakling left arm."

I opened the stall door for Lana. "Let's go make some lunch," Lana said. "I've worked up an appetite from all this ranch work."

CHAPTER 11

*A*fter a bacon, lettuce and tomato sandwich at Lana's, I headed to my house for a quick check that everyone was behaving. For the first time since I could remember, I walked inside and Ursula and Henry were having a nice, polite conversation instead of the usual heated debate. I followed the pleasantly toned voices past the dining room to the room I'd designated as the library, mostly because of the floor to ceiling bookshelves on one wall. The opposite wall consisted of large picture windows that looked out over my vast collection of unsightly weeds. Now that the restoration project had reached a room that looked out over the rear of the property, I'd begun thinking about landscaping and quiet sitting areas for my future guests. I just wasn't sure how to fund it or who to hire for the work. At the moment, I had more than enough on my hands. For now, the outdoor landscapes would just be pretty pictures in my head.

The dogs trotted ahead of me to the library. Ursula turned away from the bookshelves she and Henry had been surveying when I walked into the room. "Sunni," she said cheerily, "we weren't expectin' you, but you're right on time. Henry and I were thinking you should have these shelves sanded down to the original cherry wood and then covered with a clear coat to make them shine."

"We know just the guy to do it too," Henry said. "A friend of mine is a real Michelangelo at restoring wood."

I stared up at the weathered shelves. At one time, I was sure they'd been filled with dusty leather bound tomes. I could almost picture Edward standing in front of them, trying to decide which book to pull out. I just as quickly imagined beautiful, besotted Bonnie Ross standing next to him, reaching secretly for his hand. I shook the image from my head.

"You know, these shelves are the focal point of the room. I would love to fill them with books for the guests to read. I'll scatter some comfy reading chairs and pretty lamps throughout the room." I nodded my head. "Line up your friend, Henry. I think it's a great idea to restore them to their natural beauty."

"Woo hoo," Ursula cheered. "I told you she'd love my idea."

Henry's face bunched up, and I knew the moment of peace had ended. Even the dogs figured it out and raced out of the room. "Your idea? Ha! I thought of it and told you about it last night. You only started to agree with me this morning."

"No, Henry, as usual, you've got it all wrong," Ursula tightened the belt on her baggy overalls.

I took the change in tone as my cue to leave. I headed through to the kitchen to see if Edward was lurking about. I found him sitting on his favorite place on the hearth in the kitchen. Occasionally, I caught him in a pensive moment, where it seemed he was lost in thought. This was one of those moments. He was so distracted, he didn't notice me walk in. It was always a guess, but to me, he looked sad, almost as if he were lost and wishing he could find home.

It reminded me that I needed to check my email. Months earlier, a member of a paranormal society had given me the name of an elderly woman in New York who was a direct descendant of a man named Suffolk. Suffolk had been a distant cousin of Cleveland Ross, the man who built Cider Ridge Inn and, more notoriously, the man who had caused Edward's death. Bonnie had been whisked away to the Suffolk house when it was discovered that she was carrying Edward's baby. With a bit of research at the records office, I'd discovered that Bonnie had given birth to Edward's baby. She'd named him James Henry Milton, her family name. Henrietta Suffolk, a descendant of the family who took Bonnie in, had some information about the entire event. I'd finally gotten around to writing her an email asking if she could tell me anything about Bonnie and baby James. It was all part of an attempt to discover why Edward remained stuck at the inn, the place where he'd died. It had been two hundred years, and he was not able to move on. I was certain it had to do with his son.

I pulled out my phone to check my email.

"There you go again, staring at the thin, metal tablet. A great deal of life must pass you by while you're looking at that object." Edward floated off the hearth and drifted over to the kitchen window.

"I hardly think I'm missing a great deal of life standing in my own kitchen, and I assure you, I look at my phone very little compared to some people." He wasn't listening to me as he gazed longingly out the window. He'd lamented more than once that he missed the feel of riding a horse through a pasture or smelling the fresh cut grass on the fields. It seemed he was experiencing one of those nostalgic memories. I allowed him his silent moment of reverie and checked my email. Henrietta Suffolk had replied.

"Bingo," I said to myself, and opened the email.

Dear Ms. Taylor,

I recently went through my Great Aunt Henrietta's emails and found your request for information regarding Bonnie Louise

Milton. I'm sad to convey the news that my Great Aunt Henrietta died in her sleep last week. She was ninety-five. It was a peaceful death, and we are all grateful for that because she was a wonderful woman. As to your request for information, I coincidentally found a letter my aunt had addressed to you at the Cider Ridge Inn. It was in her letter writing desk. I dropped it at the post office yesterday, so you should be receiving it soon. I have no idea of the contents, but it seemed to contain several documents because it was quite thick. I hope that it contains what you are looking for. My aunt was a treasure trove of historical information.

    Sincerely,

    Janine Ruthbert

"Woo hoo," I cheered to myself.

Edward pulled his gaze from the window. "Did you just say woo hoo?"

"I did."

"Your exemplary vocabulary knows no bounds." It seemed he had shed his melancholy mood.

"Woo hoo is an expression of glee," I said, deciding there was no need to defend my exemplary vocabulary. "I think I might have some more information soon about James Henry Milton."

His image wavered and he appeared confused.

"Your son," I added.

"Yes, yes, I know the name. Do you think I've forgotten it already?"

"You are very changeable today. Even more so than usual. Has something happened?"

He crossed his arms and drifted back up to his perch on the hearth. "I have no idea what you mean, and no, nothing has happened other than me spending another day with that insufferable pair of nitwits."

"They are at the far end of the house, and don't forget your promise to stay out of their way." My news about James had sent him back into a darker mood. I walked closer to him. Sometimes when I neared him, I could feel the cool swirl of his aura floating around his image. It seemed especially cold today, which meant he was upset.

"Edward, it never occurred to me, but maybe you don't want me to find out more about your heir. Are you worried that I'll find bad news?"

His face shot my direction. "You mean that he was a dissolute character like his father?"

I was stunned by his statement. "Actually, I meant that he died young in some tragic accident or from illness. And you weren't dissolute."

"I was no saint, that is for certain."

"No one is . . . except maybe for a few people they call saints." Usually my humor helped lighten his mood but not this time. "If you don't want me to find out anything more, I'll stop. I just thought knowing might help you—you know—move on."

His image faded and disappeared. He reappeared at the kitchen window. "The chickadees are back at their familial nesting site," he said quietly. "That hickory tree in your front yard has been home for their nest since I walked these grounds as a real man, a human with boots that touched the ground and hands that grasped the reins of a horse bridle."

I walked to the window and scanned the tree for the tiny black-capped birds. "I never noticed them. Thank you for pointing them out." I hated to leave him in such a sad state, but I needed to get back to the carnival. "I'll see you later, Edward. Then we can talk about this again."

I turned and walked toward the doorway.

"I don't know what's waiting for me outside of this house," he said quietly.

I looked back at him. He was still watching the chickadees.

"Maybe I don't want to find out." His deep voice drifted toward the window pane.

"I understand. See, you're still far more human than you realize because that is a perfectly human reaction to something we all worry and wonder about."

He continued to gaze out the window.

"I'll see you later, Edward."

CHAPTER 12

I parked the jeep but wasn't quite ready to enter the noisy throng of carnival goers. My mind was still heavily anchored in my conversation with Edward. I'd been enthusiastically searching for the reason he was left in between worlds, and I'd never given much thought to what it meant for Edward. And to me . . . for that matter. I'd grown used to my constant, albeit, somewhat irritating, companion. Was I prepared for him to just vanish into thin air? Mostly, was I prepared to help him face his eternity, whatever that might be?

My phone rang, jarring me from my musings. There was nothing like a call from Jackson to whisk me away from dreary thoughts and back to a happy place. "Hi there."

"Hey, Bluebird, what are ya up to? I've got a spare hour. I thought we could get an ice cream."

"An ice cream break with the handsome Detective Brady Jackson is just what this disgruntled reporter needs."

"Uh oh, why disgruntled?"

Obviously, I couldn't bring up the emotional moments with the Cider Ridge ghost, but I had plenty of other things to whine about. "I'm stuck doing a story on the Spring Fair Carnival, which is about as exciting and takes as much creativity as writing a grocery list. In fact, I'm at the carnival right now. However, I haven't found the courage to climb out of my jeep yet."

"I'm just a few minutes away. I'll coax you from your vehicle and lure you into the carnival with my dashing smile and a soft serve ice cream."

"Great, my disgruntled day just turned sweeter . . . in every sense of the word. Just look for the solemn journalist in the jeep."

"I'll be there soon."

While I waited for Jackson, I took a few minutes to write a thank you and offer my sympathy to Henrietta Suffolk's great niece. I was anxious to see what she sent me but less anxious to share the information with Edward. I'd have to weigh whether or not it was in his or my best interest for him to know more about his son. Especially if Henrietta had sent bad news about little James Milton.

I took a few minutes to close my eyes and rest. It wasn't easy taking care of the farm, Lana and my own odd collection of people and ghosts central to my life. As my head cleared, the nagging notion that I had to come up with a glowing article about a less-than-glowing carnival moved to the forefront of my thoughts. I hoped to finally get an interview with Carson or his wife. Hopefully, whatever had sent them into a rage this morning had been cleared up.

A tap on my driver's side window startled me out of my rest. Jackson opened the door and I climbed out.

"Almost didn't want to bother you." He pulled me close for a kiss.

I reached up and rubbed my thumb along his jaw. "Glad you did. Otherwise, I might just have slept through the rest of the work day."

We headed toward the ticket gate. Jackson flashed his badge and that seemed to suffice for a free pass inside.

I pulled out my press pass. "Your badge works a heck of a lot better than mine. My badge usually earns me suspicious scowls."

"Trust me, so does mine." He glanced up to the sky. The earlier clouds had parted just enough to allow spots of blue, but thunder rumbled in the distance, above the mountain peaks, which meant we'd probably get rain later. "It's colder out than I thought. Do you still want ice cream?"

"Yes, it's never too cold for ice cream or too hot for cocoa. That's my motto."

We headed toward the main food aisle. "So Parker has you writing an article about the carnival, eh?"

"Yes, I have no idea what I'm supposed to say about it except that it's a carnival and a shabby, run-down one at that. Only I'm supposed to make it a glowing review because Carson Stockton is friends with the mayor."

"That's going to take some journalistic magic. Do you want vanilla or chocolate or a swirl of both?" he asked.

"Give me both. I'm feeling adventurous."

Jackson and I strolled along with our ice creams. It seemed the teenagers had woken from their alarm clock free morning, and they'd descended upon the place in droves.

"I've been grumbling on about my job, but what are you up to?" I asked. "Working on anything more interesting than a run-down carnival?"

"Nothing too riveting, just a series of unsolved bank robberies."

I nearly spurted ice cream from my nose. "Nothing too riveting? Oh my, Detective Jackson, your life is infinitely more exciting than mine. Are you getting close to catching the guys?"

"I think so. Two young guys. They've hit a few banks within a hundred mile radius. The last hit was in Smithville. They've figured out a way to block signals to the surveillance cameras, so we're going by eyewitness descriptions. We just haven't been able to match them to anyone in the police system."

"Maybe they are new to the world of crime. I have no doubt you'll catch—"

"Help! Somebody help!' The distressed yell came from behind us.

Jackson and I spun around. Carson Stockton was, once again, stumbling out of Madame Cherise's tent. Only this time there was no satisfied grin. His face was a ghostly shade of gray, and he looked close to throwing up. People began to circle the area to find out what was happening. Carson spotted Jackson and half ran toward us, trying to catch his breath as he moved clumsily through the onlookers.

"Detective," he said between gulps of air, "come quick." Jackson braced his hand under Carson's elbow to keep him from falling over. "You need to come quick, Detective Jackson. I think she's dead. I think Cherise is dead."

CHAPTER 13

*W*e had barely tasted the ice creams before we were tossing them in the trash. We left a befuddled and stunned carnival owner standing amidst a crowd of concerned visitors. I followed close at Jackson's heels as he raced to the fortune teller's tent.

He stopped just before entering. "Stay here, Sunni. Let me make sure it's safe." He disappeared inside, but curiosity got the best of me. I peeked through the slim opening between the two flaps on the tent.

There was a terrible scene inside, but it looked perfectly safe to enter. I slipped through the flaps.

Jackson opened his mouth to lecture me but then seemed to consider it a waste of breath. "Don't touch anything," he said quietly.

"Not my first time at a possible crime scene, Detective," I said with a smirk.

Cherise was slumped over, her forehead leaned against the crystal ball sitting in the center of a tiny, round table. One arm was limp to her side and the other rested lifelessly on the table over a stack of tarot cards. Blood pooled on the silver tablecloth on each side of the crystal ball and red drops flowed down the glass sphere. Jackson squatted down to get a look at Cherise's face, which was mostly hidden by hair and blood. He pulled a latex glove from his pocket and picked up her wrist to feel for a pulse. It didn't take a medical professional to know Cherise was dead. The tips of her fingers were already light blue, and her hand looked rubbery as Jackson moved it to search for signs of life.

He rested her hand on the cards and pushed to his feet.

"Carson was right," I said. "She's dead?"

"Yes, and from the looks of it, she didn't just collapse from a heart attack or stroke." He pulled out his phone. "This is Detective Jackson. I need a medical examiner and an evidence sweep team at the Stockton Traveling Carnival off Butternut Crest."

The tent flaps moved. "This is a crime scene," Jackson said before a head popped through. It was one of the uniformed officers who'd been working security detail for the carnival.

"Officer Hanson, I need you to tell Carson Stockton that he should shut down the carnival for the night. It's up to him how he wants to handle it. For now, clear a five hundred foot radius around this tent. Who's on duty with you?"

"Officer Gray," Hanson said. "She's working on getting everyone back from the scene."

"Good. The medical examiner will be here soon. Keep an eye out for his van and lead him here when he arrives." Voices rumbled outside the tent. "You'd better get out there and help Gray. Stockton made quite a scene when he stumbled out of this tent. I'm sure the entire carnival already knows about it. Oh, and, Hanson, it goes without saying, but I'll remind you anyhow—keep an eye out for anyone acting suspiciously or wearing blood splatters on their clothing."

"Yes, sir." Officer Hanson left the tent.

Jackson took a few pictures from each side of the murder

scene, while I perused the tent (without touching anything). The light was not ideal for investigating a crime scene, but the medical examiner would bring lighting equipment. It was a small space, a twelve by twelve base at the most, and Cherise had it cluttered with exotic looking lamps, vases and incense burners to create the fortune telling ambiance. Raine ran her psychic business out of her sweet, cozy house right at the end of town. Her front room was kept dark with heavy damask curtains and stained glass Victorian lampshades. But it had a certain style that worked just right for Raine's line of business. Cherise had seemed to care less about style and more about putting up props that people expected to see in a fortune teller's tent. The smell of a potent mix of incense hung in the air and seemed to permeate the canvas walls. A mahogany framed mirror hung precariously from one panel of the tent. It looked foggy from age. I walked closer and squinted at the muddled silver glass.

"Jackson, I've found something." At the bottom of the mirror, just above the wooden frame, someone had scrawled words in what appeared to be the victim's blood. "No more fortunes," I read.

Jackson walked up behind me to read the message. "I'd say that was definitely written by the killer."

I pointed at the letter f. It was a long, fancy f. The kind that almost looked like calligraphy, where the bottom of the letter curled back, making it look like the letter S with a line through it. "It's a woman." I peered up at Jackson. "The killer is a woman."

"How do you know that?"

"That fancy feminine f. It just looks like something a woman would write."

Jackson took a picture of the wording on the mirror, then looked at it closely again. "You might be right, but it's not a sure thing. Some men have nice handwriting too. Not me, mind you, but I've seen men with fancy script. But good eye, Investigator Taylor." He turned back to the table. "I'm going to lift her away from the crystal ball. Her forehead seems to be the source of the blood. Could be gory. Are you sure you want to stick around for this?"

I lifted a brow. "What do you think?"

"Right. Silly question."

He circled behind the tall chair that Cherise was sitting on. He put on gloves and pulled gently at her shoulders, not wanting to disturb any possible evidence. She fell limply back against the tall chair. Her head rested there as if she had just nodded off. My sandwich lunch tumbled in my stomach, but I managed to keep it in place. However, the tent was swirling around me a bit.

Cherise's face was covered with blood and her hair was matted with it. A large clump of it was glued to her forehead, but it was easy to spot the horrifying dent on the left side of her skull, near her temple. It had been a brutal attack, so vicious I was rethinking my earlier guess on the killer being a woman.

Jackson leaned down to get a look at the wound. "Someone struck her head with a heavy, solid object. The wound is too messy to get a clear view, but the coroner will figure out what hit her."

Jackson performed a much closer inspection of the body, and my lunch gurgled in my stomach. I turned and breathed deeply through my nostrils, taking in the stale scent of incense mixed with the metallic odor of blood.

"You all right, Bluebird?" Jackson asked, without looking up from the victim.

"Just searching for a little fresh air inside this tent. It seems to be lacking." I turned back around. "I'm fine though, just a little indigestion from the grisly scene. See anything else?" I asked.

Jackson straightened and stared down at the body. "No, it seems it just took the one blow to the head."

"Jax, remember when we saw Carson coming out of the tent yesterday with a satisfied grin?"

"Yep, and obviously he was visiting his fortune teller today too. Seems like he was quite *interested* in Madame Cherise."

"This is probably not too important," I said, "but this morning, I'd set up an interview with Carson for my piece. He was nice and accommodating on the phone. But when I arrived at his RV for the interview, Ivonne Stockton came flying out of it, filled with anger about something. She didn't say a word to me as she stormed past. I continued into the motorhome for the interview, but Carson was terse and preoccupied. He suddenly had no time for a pesky journalist. I think they had a fight."

Jackson's phone beeped. "Good to know." He answered it. "This is Jackson. All right, I'll be right out to brief the team." He lowered the phone. "The medical examiner is just pulling onto the carnival lot. I'm going out to meet them."

"Do you mind if I stay here a few minutes longer just to snoop around?" I held up my hands. "I won't touch a thing." I batted my eyelashes a few times.

"Bluebird, are you fluttering those eyelashes at me to make your case?"

I batted them again and added in a sweet smile. "Yes, is it working?"

"All right but you'll have to clear out when the coroner gets here. And don't touch anything."

I pushed my arms behind my back and clasped my hands. "I'll just use my eyes and nose. I promise."

CHAPTER 14

*A*dmittedly, I'd been braver in theory. It took me a good long minute, after Jackson left the crime scene, to get used to the idea of being alone with a murder victim. Rather ridiculous, considering I had breakfast with a dead man every morning and often shared the day's anecdotes with him in the evening. Of course, Edward was no longer flesh and bone, and more importantly, he wasn't covered in fresh blood.

Cherise was slumped against the tall back of the chair. Blood and mats of blonde hair obscured most of her face. I was grateful for that. It probably would have been less disconcerting if I hadn't sat at Lana's kitchen table with Cherise just the night before. It was always hard to swallow the notion that someone could be warm and lively and sparkling in a gold coat one minute and cold, lifeless and dead the next. It was a stark reminder of how fragile life was.

I calculated that I had only five to ten minutes before the teams of professionals streamed into the tent. It was a small enough space that I'd be in the way, so I needed to snoop around quickly. Since Jackson had done a fairly thorough survey of Cherise and the table in front of her, I decided to focus on the surroundings. I was more than happy to steer clear of the corpse.

I'd already discovered what I was sure would be a monumental clue—the words written in blood on the mirror. I circled the inside perimeter of the tent, at least where there was room to walk. I had to navigate my way around extra chairs and end tables set up with gaudy silk topped lamps. The heavy, vintage lampshades reminded me more of an old-fashioned bordello than a fortune teller's lair.

A small stack of shelves that looked as if at one point it had been nailed on a wall, leaned against the canvas. The shelves were stacked with colorful boxes of incense, patchouli, lavender, white sage. There was even a box labeled Dragon's Blood. I stepped closer to read the rest and crunched something beneath my foot. I hopped back, not wanting to get in trouble for disturbing evidence. A pile of incense sticks were strewn on the floor as if dropped suddenly. It seemed the killer might have walked in on Cherise and startled her. It was strange, considering her tent was in the center of a crowded circus. She should have been expecting customers. Unless, of course, the visitor was someone she had hoped not to see. Maybe someone she knew she'd angered. A jealous wife, perhaps?

With the exception of the one stick I broke with my shoe, I left the incense undisturbed. I circled around the table, keeping my eyes averted from the body. Like I'd bragged to Jackson, I'd been to a few murder scenes, but this one was making me uncomfortable. It might have been from standing in such close quarters with the victim or the way she was still seated at the table as if she was about to read the Tarot cards under her hand or maybe it was because I'd actually met and spoken with Cherise. Whatever the cause, I had goosebumps running along both arms. I hurried my investigation.

It seemed I hadn't needed to touch a thing. My shoes were

doing all the work today. My right foot moved freely, but my left foot was stuck to the rug beneath the table. It was a dark floral printed area rug that was faded and dirty from use. I peeled my shoe off the sticky substance on the rug and crouched down to get a closer look. I'd made a promise not to touch anything, but I saw no harm in running my fingers lightly over the sticky spot. Little nubs of worn yarn rolled under my hand as my fingertips gently adhered to a sticky substance. I lifted my fingers but couldn't smell much past the lingering odor of incense and blood.

I pushed to my feet and tapped around with my cleaner right shoe. There were more sticky spots as if someone had tracked syrup into the tent. The tent was located in the center of a carnival that was brimming with sticky treats like maple covered funnel cakes, syrup drenched snow cones, ice cream and cotton candy. Any one of Cherise's clients could have tracked it in. Only, it seemed, whoever it was had walked past the visitor's chair to the fortune teller's side of the table. Unless the stickiness came from Cherise's shoes.

I dreaded the idea and knew I'd be breaking my promise to Jackson, but I had to know if the sticky spot was a clue or just a mess left behind by the victim's shoes. I stooped back down next to the table. The shimmery silver tablecloth nearly touched the ground. I lifted it and found that Cherise liked to wear sandals just like Raine. I'd always assumed the sandals just went with Raine's colorful Bohemian style, but maybe it was a psychic thing. Either way, it made me sad to see Cherise's pale white feet resting in cute leather braided sandals. She had taken the time to paint her toe nails orange with little yellow stars. Fortunately, the position she was sitting on the chair made it so that her toes were pointed up, exposing the soles of her sandals a few inches.

I swept my finger beneath each sandal. They were gritty but not sticky.

As I pulled my head out from under the cloth, something shiny caught my eye. I knew I was breaking my promise again, but it was all in pursuit of Cherise's killer. I reached into the darkness toward the shiny speck. A teensy piece of shiny metal stuck to my fingertip. On closer inspection, I concluded that it was a piece of confetti. I ducked my head under and lifted the tablecloth higher to allow more light in. A few more pieces of shiny confetti glittered in the rug.

I scooted out from under the table but stayed crouched near the ground. There were at least a dozen pieces of confetti strewn about the rug. I pushed to my feet. Jackson and I had watched as Carson tossed an unwelcome bucket of metallic confetti on the Spring Fair Queen. Melinda had a difficult time getting it out of her hair. I would have to make a trip to the stage, where they'd crowned the queen, to see if the confetti had been cleaned up. If not, which, with the way the carnival was maintained, I felt might be the case, it meant any person walking near the stage could have picked up confetti bits on their shoes. Especially if the shoes were sticky with syrup.

Voices rumbled outside the tent, including the deep, melodic one I'd grown to recognize anywhere. The tent flap opened, ushering in the cool outside air. It suddenly beckoned me to step out for a fresh breath. Jackson seemed a little surprised and not too pleased to see me still inside the crime scene.

"I was just leaving," I said quickly.

"Too late." Jackson held the flap wider. A man and woman, each wearing white coroner coats and carrying leather bags, stepped inside. An assistant with a camera around his neck and carrying a tall, portable light followed the medical examiners.

The coroner looked confused and then askance at me. I looked to Jackson for help out of the awkward situation.

"Sunni, thanks so much for your help with keeping any curious onlookers from peeking under the tent," Jackson said calmly. He placed a hand against my back and escorted me out of the tent. I was relieved to be outside, away from the smell of blood.

"That was quick thinking, Detective Jackson," I mused. "Guess you developed that skill working for the police department."

"Nope, I learned it when I was a teenager and I needed a quick, plausible excuse for doing stuff I wasn't supposed to be doing." He led me past the team of officers waiting to go in for evidence collection.

They had done an admirable job of clearing the carnival of visitors. Even the workers had been moved out of the radius of the crime scene.

"I've got to get back in there," Jackson said. "Are you taking off?"

"Now when have you known me to just wander away from a murder investigation?"

"I haven't. I was just hoping that ten minutes in a small tent with a dead woman might have made you lose your taste for murder."

I shook my head once. "Nope. If anything, I'm more intrigued." I hopped up on my toes and kissed him lightly on the mouth. "Thank you for the ice cream. I'm sure it would have been delicious. I'll see you later, Detective Jackson."

CHAPTER 15

$\mathcal{I}$ headed toward the murmur of voices at the far end of the carnival. Apparently, it was where the carnival staff had been shepherded to when they cleared the crime scene area. I didn't see Carson or his wife amongst them. It was entirely possible that Carson was being questioned somewhere secluded to find out just what he'd discovered when he walked into Cherise's tent. It made sense that his wife would be with him at a time like this. After all, one of their regular staff members had been brutally murdered and a day's revenue had been lost. It was hard to know exactly how this event would affect attendance. With human nature being as it was, too curious when it came to the macabre and scandalous, it might very well help ticket sales. But one thing was for certain, the rest of the staff looked shaken.

Some of the women consoled each other in a huddle. There were plenty of tears and sobs and shaking heads. A green striped shirt caught my eye amidst the sea of teal and pink stripes. Calvin, this morning's unenthusiastic tour guide, paced in a small circle. His mouth was pulled tight, and he rubbed his hands anxiously together.

Since we'd shared a *wonderful bond* earlier in the day, I didn't hesitate to walk over to him. "Hello, Calvin, I noticed you look very distraught. Can I get you something? A cup of water, maybe?"

"Last person I need to talk to right now is a reporter," he barked, and marched toward a group of workers standing near the octopus ride.

"Poor Cal, he's taking it really hard," a voice said from behind.

I turned around. The girl looked exceptionally young. She was dressed in the teal and pink carnie shirt but she'd pulled on a red beanie to shield her ears from the cool air coming off the mountains.

She untied the hooded sweatshirt around her waist and pulled it on. "It's getting colder. I wonder how long the police are going to want us to wait here." She glanced at my clothes. "I think all the visitors were supposed to leave." She shrugged. "But doesn't make any difference to me if you stay." Her nametag said Brianna.

"Thanks, Brianna. I'm actually not a visitor. Well, not technically. I'm a reporter for the *Junction Times*."

"Man oh man, you reporters are fast. I bet this will make a big headline." Brianna zipped up her sweatshirt. "Poor Cherise. Is it true she was shot in the head? How come no one heard it?"

"I don't know all the details." I decided to play innocent and pretend I'd just been on the outside of it all, like the rest of them. "I did hear someone say it wasn't a gunshot."

Brianna pulled a package of gum out of her sweatshirt pocket and grinned at it as if she'd just found a twenty dollar bill. "I forgot all about this gum." She pulled out a piece and offered me one.

"No, thanks." I glanced around to see where Calvin had ended up. He had pulled himself away from the larger group that was huddled together for warmth and emotional support. Calvin had hoisted himself up on a short retaining wall that separated the Ferris wheel from the walkway. A lit cigarette jutted from his mouth. His shoulders were slumped, and he stared down at the ground. This morning, after being shooed away by Carson, I'd found Calvin and Cherise having an argument, or very heated discussion, behind the Ferris wheel. I decided to do a little digging, and gum chewing Brianna seemed like just the right person to ask.

"Brianna, you mentioned that Cal was taking it really hard. I met Calvin this morning when I was here doing interviews with staff members. I followed him around while he performed his maintenance duties." I chuckled. "I don't think he was too thrilled to have me tag along, but Carson thought it would be valuable for my article."

The gum had finally softened enough for Brianna to talk. "Ooh, you're writing an article about the carnival. How cool." Her bottom lip jutted slightly. "Carson should have sent you my way. I work at the little kiddie airplane ride. I would have been happy to answer your questions."

I'd gone on too far of a tangent from my original question, my *digging* query. I thought it was necessary for me to put some context into my short relationship with my subject of interest, namely, Calvin.

"I'm sure it would have been a much more pleasant morning than the one I spent with Calvin. He would have preferred it too. Was he especially close with Cherise?" I asked. "He seemed very upset just now when I approached him."

Brianna's brown eyes rounded with newfound interest. "That's right. You wouldn't know anything about this. It's not as if Calvin would have said anything about it on his maintenance tour."

I forced a smile and wondered if I was this hard to communicate with as a teenager. "What wouldn't I know anything about? You lost me."

Brianna leaned in close enough for me to smell the spearmint on her breath. "I've only been with the carnival for two years, but Calvin and Cherise were a thing for those two years."

I was fairly certain what 'a thing' meant, but I wanted to be sure just in case the definition for 'a thing' was different in the teenage world than the adult world.

"They were a couple?" I asked.

"Yep, hot and heavy all the way. Right up until the day when Cherise flattened him. And she didn't do it in private. The breakup was right after a staff meeting. We all heard her tell Cal she was through with him." Brianna shook her head. "I felt really bad for the guy. He was both heartbroken and humiliated." She lowered her voice. "To tell the truth, Cherise was kind of mean like that."

"That sounds pretty ruthless," I agreed. "It's hard enough to be dumped, but to have it happen in front of your coworkers—well, that's just brutal. When did this breakup happen? Was it recently?"

Brianna chewed her gum a second and considered my question. "That's right. We were down in Texas for a fair. That's when she told him they were through. It was last month. Don't remember the exact dates." She laughed. "Life on the road does that to you."

Brianna glanced back toward Calvin. He was still smoking his cigarette and avoiding conversations with others. I tried to assess what his mood was, upset, angry or indifferent. It was hard to tell.

"I think he's taking it pretty hard," I said, to see if she concurred.

"Yeah," she said. It wasn't the strong answer I expected. "It's not easy to tell with Calvin. He's kind of standoffish. He doesn't really hang out with the rest of us, and after Cherise broke it off, he became even more of a loner."

"That's too bad," I said. "Do you know why Cherise decided to break up with him? Was he treating her badly?"

"This place is like a traveling soap opera, if you know what I mean." Brianna pulled the knit beanie lower over her ears. "There are always hook ups and breakups. Most of the time, it's just out of boredom. Cherise and Calvin lasted a lot longer than most. I never talked to her much, but from what I heard, she'd fallen for someone else. I'm not sure who because if she was seeing someone, she kept it behind the scenes."

"Then Cherise might have been having a secret affair of sorts," I offered.

"Yeah, I guess that's what you'd call it. A few people were whispering around that it was Carson Stockton, the owner of the carnival. But that could just have been a rumor. Those can get pretty crazy around this place."

"I'm sure."

"Hey, Bri, come on back," a kid with bleached white hair and a tattoo scrawled around his neck called to her from the huddled group. He had his hands in his pockets, and his shoulders were hunched forward.

"That's Cody, my boyfriend," Brianna gushed. "He makes double income because he's also one of the truck drivers. You get more money if you can drive one of the bigger vehicles."

"Cody looks cold," I said.

She gave the gum a good chew. "Yeah, he lost his sweatshirt earlier. He said someone stole it while he was working the controls. He runs the Lovers' Lane ride," she gushed again. "It's considered the top job around here because it's so popular. I told him he probably just misplaced it. I mean it was just a ratty old gray sweatshirt like this one." She pulled at the edge of her hood.

"Well, I won't keep you from your friends any longer, Brianna. Thanks for talking to me."

"Sure thing. If you need a picture to go with the article—" She posed with a big smile. "Just let me know."

"I will, thanks."

Some of the other workers watched me with interest and appeared to quickly grill Brianna about the stranger she'd been talking to. My few moments with her had been enlightening, to say the least.

CHAPTER 16

The stage where the queen had been crowned and covered in confetti was closer to the center of the carnival, just past the portable buildings set up for the Lovers' Lane ride and one called Crazy Zombie World. I headed that direction.

I heard voices as I came around the Zombie World corner. While most of the carnival workers were grouped at the far end of the lot, it seemed the queen and her court had congregated near the stage. Melinda was sitting on one of the fold up chairs, and three of her friends, the same girls I'd seen with her on crowning day and this morning handing out balloons, had pulled chairs out of their rows to sit around her. Queen Melinda definitely seemed to enjoy being the center of attention, even on such a grim occasion. She had left her royal cape and crown elsewhere, which made sense considering the circumstances. It seemed her queenly duties were done for the day anyhow.

I headed through the lines of chairs set up in front of the stage and caught the eye of one of Melinda's friends, the same girl who was voicing deep concern for Melinda when they were handing out balloons. The friend leaned in and said something, and all four girls turned my direction.

"Hello," I said politely. "Don't mind me, I'm just strolling around trying to get some ideas for the article I'm writing."

"What article?" a girl with a short bob cut and big hoop earrings asked. She looked at Melinda for clarification as if being queen meant she knew exactly what I was talking about.

Melinda didn't seem to have an answer either. There was no reason she should.

I neared them. After a quick assessment, I calculated their ages between nineteen and twenty-two. I noticed that Melinda did, in fact, look quite shaken. There was still no ring on her finger either, so it was hard to tell the exact source of distress. Even as Spring Fair Queen, it was unlikely she knew Cherise personally.

I pulled out my press pass.

"The *Junction Times*," a girl with a black striped sweater and jean jacket chirped. "Are you that reporter, Sunni Taylor? My mom likes your articles, although she says sometimes you're a little too opinionated."

Being a seasoned journalist, I was always ready for a compliment or a critique. It was rare when they came together. I smiled. "Guilty as charged."

They didn't seem to understand what I meant, so I decided it was time to move on in our discussion. "I'm writing an article about the carnival—"

"And, of course you need to interview me because I was crowned queen," Melinda said with a sort of exasperated sigh. Life as a royal was apparently quite exhausting. I didn't want to embarrass her by making it seem I hadn't even considered an interview, so I went with it.

"I understand that now isn't a good time, what with everything that's happened," I said.

"Hey, wait," the friend with the hoop earrings pointed a long pink nail at me. "You're that reporter who nearly died when the horse and carriage took off through town at Christmas. And Detective Jackson jumped on and saved you."

"I saw that video," the third friend said. "I was out of town, so I missed the whole thing but everyone was sharing it." She smiled at her friends, then looked up at me. "Especially the kiss. My mom saw the video, and she said 'well, if that's what it takes to get a kiss from Detective Jackson, then I'm jumping on the next carriage'."

They broke into laughter. I found myself joining them.

"I don't recommend it as the best way to get a kiss," I said after the laughter subsided.

"Are you his girlfriend?" the girl with the black striped sweater asked. "My sister said Detective Jackson has a different girlfriend for every day of the week."

The girl with the hoop earrings, not so subtly, kicked her friend's shoe and gave her an admonishing look.

I was more than aware of Jackson's reputation with women, but I'd convinced myself it was before we started dating. Whatever he did before that was his business.

"All men are rotten," Melinda grumbled. She crossed her arms tightly and curled back against the chair. It seemed we'd landed on a sore subject. I didn't feel comfortable asking her about the engagement. I wasn't getting the same, friendly, happy-to-talk about anything vibe I had gotten from Brianna. And I wasn't terribly interested in Melinda's social life. I was focusing on Cherise's murder.

"Did any of you girls know Cherise?"

My question started a circle of secretive glances between the friends, Melinda included.

"Why do you ask?" Melinda asked curtly.

"No reason. I was just wondering what happened to her. Have you heard anything?" I added casually.

The girl with the hoop earrings seemed to be the unofficial

spokesperson for the group. "We don't know anything. We were on the other side of the carnival, by the rides. Melinda was handing out free balloons, and we were all helping her. "

"Yes, after we spent a good half hour looking for Melinda's cape," the girl in the sweater complained.

The girl with the earrings rolled her eyes at being interrupted and continued with her story. "So, we were handing out balloons. Then we heard a lot of commotion and saw people heading toward the game area. A few minutes later, Carson and some of the workers were walking around telling visitors that the carnival would be closed for the rest of the day."

"But you girls stayed behind?" I asked.

Melinda seemed put off by my question. "We weren't visitors. I'm the Spring Fair Queen," she reminded me with a snooty chin lift. "My friends were helping me."

"Of course, yes, that makes sense," I said, although it really didn't.

"What does it matter now," Melinda's haughty tone had disintegrated. "My whole reign as queen is ruined. The carnival is a disaster. This week was supposed to be the best week of my life." She covered her face for a few sobs. Her friends immediately leapt into comfort mode.

"You don't know if the carnival is ruined," the girl with earrings said. "They'll probably open up tomorrow like nothing happened."

It seemed like a rather cold assessment of the situation but then they were working hard to ease their friend's distress. If my suspicions were correct, that Sutton Wright had proposed and then just as quickly withdrawn the offer, then it truly was a bad week for Melinda.

"Well, take care," I said. "And I hope your week gets better." I headed off.

"I'll probably be more in the mood for an interview and pictures tomorrow," Melinda called as I walked away. Apparently, terrible week or not, the Spring Fair Queen didn't want to miss out on having her wise words and picture in the paper.

"Sounds good," I waved. I was determined to search the stage area for a few pieces of confetti. I needed to make sure it was the same metallic tidbits I'd found in the rug of Cherise's tent.

The girls were deep in conversation and didn't seem to care or notice that I was snooping around the stage. Of course, they had no idea that I was investigating the murder. I circled the portable steps that led up to the stage and scanned the ground for confetti. A day had passed since the crowning ceremony and plenty of feet had tracked through the area since then, distributing dirt and debris and carrying away anything like confetti that tended to stick to surfaces like shoes. Fortunately, metallic glitter was easy to spot, even under a dimly lit sky. Three silver particles sparkled up at me from the black rubber mats on the bottom step. I pulled a tissue from my coat pocket and stooped down to sweep them up. They were made of the same material as the confetti on Cherise's rug. I folded the pieces into my tissue and put them in my pocket. It wasn't any kind of earth shattering discovery. Just about anyone who walked near the stage area could have picked up confetti on their shoe and carried it into Cherise's tent, but I was going to hold onto the pieces just in case they were significant.

My work done, I decided to head back toward the crime scene and look for Jackson. With any luck, he'd be willing to share new details about the murder.

CHAPTER 17

*J*ackson was standing outside Cherise's tent talking to Officer Inez Reed. She was a gun expert, extremely skilled, according to Jackson. She was also beautiful with dark copper hair and a smooth, olive complexion. The latter, I'd deduced on my own because it was as plain as the perfect symmetry of her face. She came to most crime scenes. I always had to work a bit to not be jealous that she often worked closely with Jackson. It seemed, I'd let Melinda's friend's comment get under my skin a little more than I realized. My track record with men didn't exactly make me a steel statue of confidence.

Officer Reed spotted me first. She glanced my direction and said something to Jackson. He turned around. The smile that broke on his face made all the negative thoughts flutter away. Jackson walked over to meet me, and Officer Reed went back inside the crime scene.

"Well, Inspector Taylor, did you find anything relevant?" He leaned forward and kissed my nose. "That little button nose is cold. You should head home."

"Eventually. Did your team find anything?"

"I asked you first," he reminded me.

"I talked to one of the carnival workers, a nice girl named Brianna who runs one of the kiddie rides. She told me that Calvin, the maintenance man, who I just happened to spend the morning with, had been in a long relationship with Cherise. Apparently, she made quite a show of ruthlessly breaking up with him right in front of their coworkers. I asked him if he was all right or if I could get him something, and he nearly bit my head off."

"You spent the morning with him?" he asked. He was especially cute with a furrowed brow.

"Really? That's the part that stands out to you? I told you I was doing interviews for my article. When Carson was too out of sorts to talk this morning, he sent me to shadow Calvin on his maintenance rounds. I think he wanted me to put in a good word about his highly maintained, super-safe carnival rides."

"That's right. Sorry. Got a little hot under the collar when you said you'd spent the morning with someone named Calvin."

I smiled. "Yeah? Hot under the collar?"

"Never mind that. Sounds like good information. I'll tell Officer Reed. She's taking over this case."

The tent flaps lifted and a woman wearing a white coroner's coat emerged. She turned and grabbed hold of the end of a gurney. We watched, in silence, as Cherise's body was wheeled out of her tent and into the back of the coroner's van.

"Coroner said she's been dead anywhere from two to three hours," Jackson said. "So Carson found her fairly soon after the murder."

"Doesn't leave a big window of time. He had to have been her first *visitor* after the killer." I turned back to Jackson. "Why is Officer Reed taking over?"

"I'm still working on this bank robbery. It's a priority right now. The two thieves are getting more brazen, and they're carrying guns."

I sensed that the bank robbery case was getting to him. It was rare for him to get frustrated, but I could see it in the set of his jaw.

"I'm sure you'll catch them soon," I said. I was disappointed he wasn't going to be working the murder case. It meant no good insider information.

"I don't think they're local boys," he said.

"Boys? Are they that young?"

"Early twenties at the most. The best lead I've got is that one of them is wearing shoes that have lights. They flash when he takes a step." He took a deep breath and raked his hair back with his fingers. "Anyhow, I'm off this case for now. I'll let Officer Reed know about the maintenance man's relationship with the victim. I'm sure she'll start interviewing some of the carnival workers soon. Carson said he was going to have them get to work cleaning up for the day once the coroner was finished and gone. Speaking of the maintenance man, they found the murder weapon. Carson said it was a tool that belonged to the carnival." Jackson motioned for me to follow him to a fold out table that had been set up outside the crime scene. Evidence bags of every shape and size were carefully laid out on the table.

One of the smallest bags contained a few pieces of the metallic confetti. Another contained what appeared to be fibers from the rug under Cherise's table.

"I see your team has found the confetti and the sticky spots on the rug," I said, with a smug grin. "I noticed both of those things in my quick perusal of the crime scene."

"You definitely have a knack for snooping out evidence." There was a touch of pride in his voice.

"Thank you." I moved down the table to the large bag that contained the mirror with the cryptic message 'no more fortunes' written in blood. I shrugged. "Of course, any amateur could have found this piece of evidence. I wonder if the murderer just got carried away in the heated moment and scrawled the sentiment? Or maybe the words have a hidden meaning?"

"Not too sure," Jackson said. "Like you already noted, the unique way they wrote the letter f might lead us to the killer. Once they narrow down a suspect list, they can request some hand-writing samples to look for a match." He moved to the last bag on the table, an extra large one that contained a long metal rod with a triangular shaped head. The blood-smeared, thick metal triangle contained what looked like cylindrical teeth. "This was the murder weapon."

"That definitely looks like a one blow kind of weapon. And with those teeth protruding from the end, I'd say it wouldn't even take all that much strength to crush a skull."

"Nope, wouldn't take much at all."

I leaned closer to get a better look at the object. "I don't proclaim to be a tool expert, but Henry and Ursula have an impressive collection of them. I haven't ever seen anything like this one."

"They wouldn't have any need for this. It's called a Hickey bar."

I chuckled. "Oh wow, I'll bet that thing really leaves a good sized hickey."

"Funny lady. It's used to bend rebar. Carson said they use it to straighten out crooked tracks on the rides. Your information about the maintenance man might be the best we've gotten yet. He would certainly have easy access to the tools."

"Its seems my sleuthing skills know no bound."

"About that, Sunni—" Jackson's voice grew sterner.

"Uh oh, why do you sound like my dad used to when he was about to tell me I was grounded."

Officer Reed came out of the tent with another small evidence bag. I stretched up and tried to look past Jackson to see what she had, but he took hold of my hand and led me away from the table and the activity near the tent. He continued around the baseball throw booth, where I'd brilliantly won him a stuffed unicorn, and out of sight of the others.

He lifted my chin so I had no option except to look right at him. Not that that was ever a bad thing, but I sensed he was working up to a lecture about what I liked to call my parallel investigation.

His amber eyes took on that dark gold glow that came on whenever he was in a serious mood. "You've spent some time checking out clues today, but now you need to step away from this murder."

I stared up at him for a long, quiet moment. Then a laugh shot from my mouth.

He dropped his finger and shook his head. "As you might recall, my little Bluebird, you nearly got yourself killed at Christmas when you stepped into a murder investigation. People who kill other people are not in their right minds. Simply put, they are dangerous."

"I do recall the harrowing incident. I also recall that it earned me a kiss."

"Well, it nearly earned me a heart attack. Sunni, promise me you won't do anything dangerous. I'm not even on this case, so I won't be able to swoop in on my horse to rescue you." He paused and seemed to be reliving that day.

"You've got to admit," I said, "that was actually pretty darn cool, wasn't it?"

"Except for the part where you nearly got killed," he reminded me.

"True, that part wasn't so great." I placed my hands on his chest and leaned closer to him, instantly basking in his cozy body heat. "I'll just interview a few people and get a sense of how they felt about Cherise. I am, after all, tasked with writing a story about the carnival."

He wrapped his arms around me to bring me even closer against him. "I thought Seymour wanted you to write a glowing review."

"He does but he never said anything about leaving out murder." I smiled up at him. "Now about that kiss."

CHAPTER 18

*J*ackson left the scene, reluctantly, knowing that I was still snooping around. I assured him I wouldn't do more than ask the other carnival employees a few questions, here and there. The days were getting longer, but the late afternoon clouds had made it seem as if the sun had already set. It was a brisk spring evening, and a dismal mood hung over the carnival like a cold, wet blanket.

I lingered near the remaining police activity. Most of them had seen or met me at some point in my relationship with Jackson, and they didn't seem to mind that I hung around. Cherise's body had long since been removed. A still shaken Carson Stockton was talking to Officer Reed. It seemed he had plans to reopen the carnival the next morning. He just couldn't afford not to, were the words I overheard. He was concerned that the tent, now roped off with yellow caution tape, would be sitting in the center of the carnival. Not the ideal centerpiece for a spring fair. While they worked out the details of what to do with the literally pop-up crime scene, I headed in the direction of a woman's voice being broadcast through a megaphone. I'd only heard her a few times, but I was certain it was Ivonne Stockton. It dawned on me then that I had yet to see Ivonne during the chaotic past few hours.

"Everyone, please gather in front of the stage," Ivonne announced as she walked down the main aisle that led through the rides. Half the workers were already sitting in some of the metal chairs. Melinda and her friends were no longer sitting near the stage. They weren't paid employees of the carnival, so there was no need for them to stick around.

Ivonne Stockton reminded me of Miss Rutherford, my tenth grade softball coach, with a megaphone in one hand and a clipboard in the other. The only thing missing was Miss R's silver whistle and her ramrod straight posture. Ivonne was also shorter and a little softer in the middle and arms than my coach.

"Everyone, sit," she ordered. "The faster we get started, the earlier you can be off for the night. It's been a long, trying day, and I'm sure you all want to get to your trailers to rest.

A weary, muttering crowd of about thirty carnies shuffled to the chairs with sweatshirts and coats covering up the signature teal and pink shirts. Ivonne was the only person who still looked sharp and fresh as if she had just started her day. She seemed a little too *lively* considering what had just happened in the middle of her carnival, especially in contrast to the rest of her crew.

"Quickly, quickly take a seat." She gave her last order through the megaphone and then turned it off as the group quieted to a low mutter and eventual silence.

I stayed off in the shadows hoping to hear the entire meeting without anyone taking notice. I scanned the group for Calvin and spotted him in the last row at the end. He was slumped down with rounded shoulders and arms crossed tightly. His chin was nearly touching his chest. It didn't take a body language reading expert to see that he was clearly trying to withdraw from everything happening around him.

"I know it's been a terrible afternoon, and it will take all of us a great deal of time to get over what has happened," Ivonne started. "Cherise was a good friend, and we'll miss her."

"Do the police know what happened?" someone called out from the chairs.

"They're working on it. Hopefully, we'll have some answers soon. There were a lot of people milling about at that time, our busiest part of the day, so I'm sure it will take them awhile to sort it all out. In the meantime—" she whisked off to a different topic, seemingly anxious to leave the last one behind. "I know it's hard after such a great shock, but if you could all return to your stations and clean up for the night, just as you would for any regular closing. That means getting everything ready for tomorrow."

"We're going to be open tomorrow?" a woman called. A disgruntled murmur moved through the group.

"Thought we'd at least have a day off," someone else said to a few agreeing cheers.

"Out of respect to Cherise," someone else offered.

Ivonne waited for the murmurs and sidebar conversations to stop. "Yes, all of your comments make sense, only how many of you can miss an entire day of pay? We can't pay you if the carnival isn't open. We're already losing money this afternoon."

More disgruntled mumbles and a few head shakes. "Seems like we deserve a paid day off after what we've been through," someone else said.

Ivonne patiently waited for them to finish the next round of complaints. This round took longer and seemed to be growing steam, instead of falling off. She lifted the megaphone, then seemed to think better of it. Yelling at the group through a speaker wasn't going to help them see her side of things. It was a typical management versus workers kind of dispute.

Ivonne lowered the megaphone and lifted her hand, teacher fashion, to stop the talking. "I understand why you're upset. The best I can do is offer two hours of bonus pay for working tomorrow. But closing down for another full day will not only put us in violation of the contract we have with the town but the financial hit will mean cutting back on budgetary necessities like hot dog buns and paper cups. That's all I have to say. Please head back to your stations, clean up and prepare to open in the morning. The sooner you get started, the sooner you can be off for the night to reflect and recover from this terrible day." With that, she turned sharply on her heels to let them know she was done and they could continue to complain amongst themselves or get finished with their work for the evening.

The grumbles and groans continued for a few minutes after Ivonne left the area, but, slowly, they started heading toward their stations to finish their work. I had my eye on the kid who ran the baseball game booth. It was located right next to Cherise's tent. He was my first logical choice for an interview.

My only interaction with the guy, a lanky kid of eighteen or nineteen, was when I won the unicorn at his stand with one good throw of the baseball. His comment about my age had made it easy to remember him. I followed casually behind as he lumbered on long, thin legs toward his game booth. He stopped short, seemingly not expecting to see the yellow tape draped around Cherise's tent. The woman who ran the ring toss on the opposite side was equally stunned. They both stopped side by side and stared at the yellow tape as it dangled and drooped in the breeze. The evidence team had cleared away most of the equipment, along with the bags of evidence and the bloody murder weapon.

Officer Reed and Officer Hanson were finishing up a few details with Carson. I'd hung back behind the two carnies, so I couldn't hear what was being discussed. I was certain it had to do with the removal of Cherise's tent. A few of the other workers came around the corner behind me. Their conversation fell off as they spotted the yellow tape.

"It's just like in the movies," one girl said to the guy next to her.

"You never think it's going to happen and then boom, you're standing in the middle of a murder scene."

The baseball guy recovered from his shock at seeing the yellow tape and circled to the back of his booth. He ducked under the table that held some of the toy prizes and popped up inside. The two officers followed Carson in the direction of the RVs, so I was in the clear.

The baseball guy started straightening out the prizes on the table and wall, filling in spaces where a prize had been removed. He didn't see me walk up. The sound of my throat clearing startled him. He spun around holding one of the unicorns in his hand, apparently ready to heave it if necessary.

"I'm so sorry. I didn't mean to startle you," I said. "Especially under the circumstances." He had a sweatshirt on but it was unzipped. His badge said Tad. "I know you've got some work to do, but I'm with the *Junction Times*. I was hoping you could answer a couple of questions."

His forehead folded up. "Hey, you're that lady with the good arm. The one who won the unicorn with one throw."

"Yes, that's right." I suppressed a grin. It had been a number of years since I'd heard someone say I had a 'good arm'. "Nice that you remembered."

"Well, not that many older ladies can throw like that."

"Should have stopped while I was ahead," I muttered under my breath. "Anyhow—" I looked pointedly at his nametag. "Tad, I was wondering if you could answer a few quick questions."

His bony shoulders jerked with a shrug. "Don't know why you'd bother but go ahead. I'm going to keep cleaning."

"Of course. I don't mind. Did you happen to notice anyone hanging around Madame Cherise's tent? Someone who might not normally be there?"

He squeezed a stuffed dragon in his hand and hung it up on the wall behind him. Then he turned back to me. "I thought you were going to ask about carnival stuff. I didn't know you were here about the murder."

"Yes, well, I am writing an article about the carnival," I said slowly to give myself time to come up with a good reason for my question. "It's just that—well, let's face it. Everyone in town already knows about it, so they'll expect to see it mentioned when I do the write up on the carnival."

"Guess that makes sense." He shuffled some of the toys around so matching animals were grouped together. "I wasn't really watching Cherise's tent. I mean, why should I? I've got my own booth to run. She had some customers, you know. People I didn't know. I saw Calvin working on something behind the tent. I think it was the generator for the lights. Sometimes it goes out and then Cherise is in the dark." His face dropped. "I mean was in the dark." He went back to stacking prizes. "I've seen the boss, Carson, going in there a few times this week. Not sure what was happening." He chuckled. "Unless he was getting his fortune read. Anyhow, it got pretty busy, so I didn't really notice who else went inside the tent."

"Yes, I was here getting ice cream earlier, and it was crowded. I'm sure everyone was disappointed the day ended so abruptly."

"Yeah, well, they can come back tomorrow. Carson is making us open up. Seems like we should have gotten at least one day off." Tad started stacking the milk bottles for tomorrow's first game. He was just angry enough about the lack of a day off to clank them together as he built them into a pyramid.

"Yes, I'm sure everyone needs some time to recuperate from the shock," I said.

"Everyone but Ivonne and Carson, apparently. You'd think they just had a ride break down instead of one of the carnies killed." He waved his thin arm toward the tent. "And right in the middle of the whole darn place."

I had never run a business like the Stocktons', but it did seem that they were being cold about the whole thing. They might

CALAMITY AT THE CARNIVAL

regret their decision when they had a spring fair carnival being run by a grim looking, grumpy group of employees.

"Did you know Cherise well?" I asked.

"We've been working side by side for three years, so yeah, I knew her well. I mean we didn't hang out after hours or anything. She's kind of old for us to be buddies, you know." Cherise was thirty, at the most.

"Naturally, those of us in the older generation don't enjoy the same things as you young people," I said with a pretty good imitation of an old granny. The sarcasm went right past him. "Thanks for taking the time to talk to me, Tad."

"Sure thing." He returned his full attention to cleaning up his game booth. There were a few other people I could talk to but I needed to head out.

There were hungry farm animals waiting for their Aunt Sunni.

CHAPTER 19

$\mathcal{M}$y phone rang just as I reached the jeep. "I left two voicemails," Emily said with unusual irritation in her tone. "Why didn't you call me back?"

"I'm sorry, Em. I was on assignment, so I'd muted my phone. What's up? Are you guys having a romantically good time?" I opened the car door and climbed inside.

"How come you didn't tell me about Lana?" Emily was rarely this upset.

"Uh, because I didn't want to ruin your time away. I'm sorry." I heard chickens clucking in the background. "Where are you? I hear chickens."

"Yes. Those are my chickens. Hold on." There was some shuffling and more clucking. "Out, King Harold, right now, you scoundrel," Emily snapped. She got back on the phone. "Nick woke up with a sore throat, so we decided to head back early. That was on the voicemail I left you."

"Again, I apologize. I was just about to head to your house to feed the critters, but I guess I'll just go straight to Lana's to check on her."

Soft bleating sounds came through the phone.

"Are those my girls?" I asked. "Have they been saying good things about me?"

Emily's tone lightened. "Yes, they said Auntie Sunni took good care of them. I'm making an artichoke frittata and corn muffins to take to Lana's for dinner. Nick took his cup of tea and honey and crawled into bed, so I figured I'd spend some time with her. I'll see you when I get there. What assignment were you on that kept you from answering your phone?"

"It started as a dull story about the Spring Fair Carnival," I said.

"Oh, that shabby, run-down thing." It was rare for Emily to be negative, even about shabby, run-down carnivals. It was obvious she was upset that not only had her nice trip been cut short by Nick's sort throat but then she came home to discover that Lana had been hurt and we'd kept it secret from her. To add insult to injury, I'd ignored my phone for a good three hours.

"It definitely needs, as they say, 'a new coat of paint'," I said. "And now, it seems they'll be looking for a fortune teller."

Emily paused. "Did you say a fortune teller?"

I started the jeep. "Yes, their usual psychic, Madame Cherise, was murdered."

Emily's sigh fizzled through the phone. "Jeez, Sunni, why are you always stepping into the middle of a murder?"

"I don't know. Just lucky I guess," I quipped.

"And weird and kooky and a little ghoulish," she added. "I've got to check on my frittata and my patient. I'll see you at Lana's."

"All right. Tell Nick I hope he feels better soon. And bring extra butter for those corn muffins. Lana's fridge was looking kind of empty this morning."

"I better stop by the store on the way. See you soon."

I made a quick stop home to pick up the dogs. I'd been neglecting them for the past few days, and I was sure they'd like to see Lana and Emily. Henry and Ursula had already packed up for the evening. I had to admit, I was relieved not to see Henry's truck in the driveway. It had been a long day, and I was tired and hungry. I was equally glad not to see Edward, especially after his sullen mood this afternoon. He was most likely still lurking around the empty rooms on the second story, where he stayed when he was trying to keep clear of Ursula and Henry.

Redford and Newman trotted ahead to the jeep and climbed into the backseat. They were both smiling from ear to ear, like two little kids heading out for an adventure. I pulled onto the dirt road that connected the three properties, Lana's house, the Cider Ridge Inn and Emily's farm. The first heavy drops of a cold spring rain hit the windshield as I drove to Lana's. Headlights flashed behind me as I drove up to her house. Raine pulled up right after me.

I opened the back door. The dogs jumped out and loped up the porch steps, anxious to see Lana. I waited for Raine to get out of her car.

"Oh my gosh, did you hear?" she said before both feet were even on the ground. She had a bottle of wine tucked under her arm. "Cherise Duvay has been killed." She slammed her car door shut. She took a step but was yanked back as she quickly discovered that she'd caught the edge of her skirt in the door. "Gosh darn this skirt. Happens every time."

I took hold of the wine so she could free herself from the car. "Isn't that crazy? I can't believe it," she continued.

We walked toward the house.

"You already knew, didn't you?" she asked.

I smiled weakly. "I was there when Carson found her."

"See, that's the one drawback about having a best friend who is also the local reporter. You never miss a headline. In fact, I'd say it's downright astonishing how you just always happen to be in the vicinity when someone gets murdered."

"Emily said almost the exact same thing. She told me I was ghoulish for being delighted about my good luck." We reached the front door. I used my key. Newman and Redford pushed their noses through and burst into the house.

"Lana, beware, there's a couple of very excited pups on their way to see you," I called into the house. "I don't want them to jump on her," I said to Raine.

Lana was talking in her 'auntie loves her puppies' voice. The boys were already happily gnawing away on treats by the time Raine and I reached the kitchen. My sister looked way better than she had the night before and this morning. It seemed the initial shock and pain of the break were wearing off. There were four red checkered placemats and silverware set on her kitchen table. She was balancing four plates on her good hand.

I put the wine down on the counter and took the plates from her. "Why didn't you wait for us?" I asked. "You're already trying to do too much."

"I was bored so I decided to set the table." She pulled out a chair and sat down. "But now that you guys are here, I'll let you do the rest. And I'll take a glass of that wine."

Raine took care of the wine, and I got the glasses down from the cupboard.

"We are in big trouble with little sis for keeping my accident secret," Lana said.

I placed a glass on each placemat. "I know. I made things worse by not answering my phone all afternoon. I had no idea they were on their way home. I finally answered a call, and an unusually stern Emily was on the other side of it."

I sat down across from Lana. "We were just trying not to ruin her weekend. I'm sure she won't stay upset for long. She is bringing us one of her butter and egg dream frittatas."

"And her corn muffins," Lana added in gleefully. "I would have done one of those frantic, fast clap things to show just how excited I am about the muffins but it's impossible to show joy, in any form, with a mega wrap on my arm. I hope the permanent fiberglass cast will give me a little more freedom to move my fingers."

"I wouldn't count on it." Raine poured the wine. "I broke my right arm in middle school, and I couldn't even write my name."

I looked up at her. "How did you break your arm? Or should I ask?"

"Considering it's me, it was actually a pretty normal, cut and dry kind of arm break. I was carrying my lunch tray to a table, and I couldn't see over the darn thing. Tripped on a stupid backpack. Food tray flew up, macaroni and cheese sprayed everywhere and my right arm, bravely and stupidly, decided it could stop the fall all by itself."

"Ouch," Lana scrunched up her nose. "My arm hurts just thinking about it."

"Hello," Emily called from the front door. Newman and Redford hopped to their feet and raced to greet her.

"Emi, big, silly dogs coming your way," I called. I would not forgive the two clowns if they knocked the corn muffins or frittata out of her hands. I was starved and my tummy was set on both.

Raine and I got up to help her carry in the food. Emily handed me the basket of corn muffins. She handed Raine a grocery bag filled with goodies for Lana's refrigerator.

"I've got to go back to the car and get the frittata," Emily said.

"Do you need me to get anything else?" I asked.

"Nope, I'll be right back." Emily walked out.

Raine and I carried the food to the kitchen. "Do the police have any idea about who might have killed her?" she asked.

"Who got killed?" Lana asked, hearing just the tail end of Raine's question.

"You didn't hear?" Raine was practically tripping over herself with excitement. "Finally. I never get to break any interesting news to Miss Nose-in-Everything Reporter over here." Raine made a detour from the refrigerator and stopped at the table with the bag of groceries so she could give Lana the full story, even though she knew very few of the details.

"You know that woman I brought over here last night, Cherise Duvay, the fortune teller?" Raine started and, of course, her long introduction was going to give away the surprise ending.

Lana sat up with interest. "Someone killed her?"

Raine's posture deflated. "You knew too?"

"Know, goofy, you walked into the kitchen talking about someone being killed. Then you brought up your friend. It's called putting two and two together," Lana said.

"Yeah, I guess I should have started with the gritty stuff." Raine trudged dejectedly to the refrigerator to put away the groceries.

The delicious scent of Emily's buttery frittata floated in, and we all stopped to take a deep breath. Emily stepped into the kitchen wearing two blue oven mitts and carrying the cast iron pan as if it were filled with priceless jewels. Her thick blonde hair was tied back with a red bandana, and her cheeks were stained pink from the sun. "It's still hot, even after my quick trip into the grocery store."

"Did you stop at the store?" Lana asked. "You are the most wonderful sister a girl could have."

I cleared my throat to remind her I was standing just a few feet away.

Lana laughed. "And you are too, Sunni."

"That sounded as forced as when you had to tell Aunt Winifred that the itchy wool sweater she knitted you was your absolute favorite." I sat down to drink my wine and nibble a corn muffin.

"Oh my gosh, I forgot all about that sweater. I had to wear it at Christmas for two years until I finally grew out of it." Lana reached for a muffin. "That thing was pure misery."

Emily placed the cast iron pan on a trivet in the center of the table and cut the frittata into slices. With the yummy food served, Emily and Lana peeled off into a conversation about how Lana got hurt and everything the doctor said. I used it as my chance to ask Raine a few questions about Cherise.

"Hey, Raine, do you think Cherise had a lot of enemies?"

Raine slathered butter on a muffin. "Not that I know of, but then I didn't know her all that well. She had been dating someone at the carnival, but she mentioned that he was far too clingy and she broke it off." I tried to picture Calvin as clingy but just couldn't visualize it. "She did say that she and the owner of the carnival didn't get along at all."

That deflated my theory about the affair. "So, she didn't care for Carson Stockton?"

"No, not Carson." Raine licked the butter from her fingertip. "Carson's wife. I think her name starts with an I or a V. I can't remember what she said."

"Ivonne," I offered.

"Yes, that's the name. Cherise said she was worried she might get fired and figured the only reason she still had a job was because Carson liked her." She looked over at my sister. "Emi, this frittata is melting in my mouth."

"It's delicious, Em. No wonder you're Lana's favorite sister." I winked at Lana, who rolled her eyes in response.

I turned my focus back to Raine. "Do you think it's possible that Carson liked Cherise a little too much?" I asked.

Her glasses slid down her nose. She pushed them back up. "What do you mean?"

"You mentioned that you thought she was seeing a married man. Could it be she was having an affair with her boss?"

"Who's having an affair?" Lana asked. "The conversation is way better at your end of the table. Enough about broken bones and husbands with sore throats. Who are you talking about?"

"Cherise, my friend who was murdered," Raine said, before a casual bite of her food.

Emily's eyes rounded. "Your friend was murdered?"

"The psychic, Madame Cherise," I filled in the information. "The victim I told you about on the phone."

"She was having an affair?" Lana obviously wanted to get back to the more scandalous part of the story.

"I think so," Raine said, and then answered my earlier question. "I suppose it just might have been her boss. Although, he's a good fifteen years older than her." She snapped her fingers. "Maybe that's why Ivonne didn't like Cherise."

"Makes sense to me," I said. "The question is—if Ivonne knew about the affair, was she mad enough to commit murder?"

CHAPTER 20

I turned off the hair dryer and heard the distinctive sound of my microwave beeping. Someone was in my kitchen, and unless Edward had suddenly decided that two hundred years of perpetuity had made him hungry, I surmised that Ursula and Henry had arrived early.

I took one last look in the mirror for no real reason. It wasn't as if I was going to adjust or add anything to my appearance. Ursula was in full lecture mode by the time I reached the kitchen. Henry had sat himself down with the leftover chunk of frittata I'd brought home. He was drowning it in ketchup.

"That is one of those fry tots," Ursula said. "You don't cover it with ketchup. What barn were you raised in?"

"The one with the loud, bleating sheep," Henry answered calmly. "Oh wait, that was you." He plunged his fork into the ketchup and eventually struck egg. "Morning, Sunni. Hope you don't mind." He lifted the fork of food. "Our stove broke last week, and I was tired of cold cereal."

Ursula shook her head. "Well, if you'd fix the darn thing, we could cook something up." She headed to the microwave. The bottoms of her overalls were rolled up high enough to expose a pair of pink and black checked stockings. Ursula turned around with a corn muffin on a plate. "I thought this muffin would be better warm," she said.

Edward sat on the kitchen hearth watching the whole scene with his usual disgust. I shot him an admonishing look, reminding him about our agreement.

"This egg is delicious," Henry said as he dug back in for more.

"It sure is. Emily made it. Have you talked to your friend about restoring the bookshelves?" I asked.

Henry tapped the table. "I knew there was something I needed to do."

"Do you mean to tell me you that you forgot to call him?" Ursula's screech was enough to make Edward vanish.

"That's all right, Henry," I said, now regretting that I'd brought it up. "It's no hurry." I poured myself a cup of coffee and headed out onto the front steps to drink it. I needed peace and quiet to plot my next move and to think about what I'd learned so far. I sat down and settled in with my hot cup of coffee.

My peace was, of course, instantly interrupted. "I don't understand why we must tolerate them at meal time, especially breakfast."

I glanced back at Edward. He was perched on the front window ledge, his long legs and the permanent black boots dangled in the air.

"Since when are you concerned about meal time being interrupted?" I returned to my coffee and the sunbathed view of my front yard, which was mostly overgrown grass and tall weeds. Still, they looked spectacular with bits of dew left behind by the rain.

"They arrive early and partake of your food, without asking. I caught the longing look you cast that egg tart before that imbecile drowned it with the tomato sauce."

I nodded. "It's true. I was planning on heating that up for my dinner, but they work hard when they're here. And they do good work, so I have no complaints."

Edward coasted to the edge of the top step, his invisible fence on the property. The poor soul wasn't even allowed to step out and remember what it felt like to have the sun shower him with warmth and light.

"You came out here to get away from them," he said. It was a statement and not a question.

"You got me there," I confessed. "I've got some things on my mind, and it's a little hard to concentrate in the same room with Ursula."

"You don't say," he said wryly. "What things do you have on your mind? Not that man with the—"

"If you say unkempt man with the wild hair one more time, Edward, I'm going to throw this coffee at you."

"You could try, but I'm afraid it wouldn't be terribly effective. I won't call him unkempt anymore. You have my word. How about rumpled or bedraggled or maybe disheveled?"

"Don't you have some place to be, Edward?"

"Where on earth would I have to be?" he asked.

"I don't know, some place other than out here thinking up words to describe my boyfriend."

"Boyfriend," he scoffed. "That's ridiculous. You need to endure a much longer courtship to even consider him more than an acquaintance."

"I think we passed the acquaintance requirements already. Anyhow, I wasn't thinking about Jackson." I stood and walked up to the top step where he lingered, his feet just an inch from the ground. I'd already calculated that Edward must have been six foot two or three when he was alive. "A woman died at the carnival yesterday. I'm trying to figure out who might have killed her."

I was always amazed how someone who was mostly vapor, and sometimes very frail wavering vapor at that, could make such direct eye contact. It was another thing I'd deduced about the man. Edward Beckett must have been one of those people who had no problem looking others directly in the eye. I pictured him as a highly confident man who lived life to the fullest and didn't care what people thought of him. It was probably the reason for him always getting into trouble and eventually finding himself dead from a gunshot wound.

"You do spend your day in the most bizarre fashion," Edward said. "Why are you always trying to chase down cutthroats and assassins?"

I was relieved that yesterday's topic of Edward's eventual move into eternity was not front and center today. It was an awkward and emotional topic that was sometimes better to ignore.

"I'm not chasing them down. I'm merely looking for information to make my writing more memorable." I laughed at my own reasoning. "But the chase is sort of fun too."

"Well, let's hear all about it. I could use some fun before I have to spend the day with the two nitwits again." He seemed genuinely interested, and it was my opportunity to relay some of the details aloud to see if anything stood out."

"There's a traveling carnival in town for spring break." I stopped. "Guess you wouldn't know much about them. They started about a hundred years after—well, you know."

"After my death?" he asked. "You needn't tiptoe around the subject. I'm well aware that I'm dead."

I laughed. "I suppose that secret is out, yes. Anyhow, the carnival has games where you can win big stuffed toys, and greasy foods that will stay and torment your stomach for days after you ingest them and wild, twisting rides that can occasionally make you lose the food so that you don't have to suffer with it for days." I couldn't help but smile about my description of a carnival.

"You modern day folk entertain yourselves in the strangest ways. It doesn't sound too outlandish to think that someone died at this traveling carnival. I rather wonder if anyone would survive after such an ordeal."

"I might have over exaggerated a little. Generally, people, especially kids, enjoy their time at a carnival. Anyhow, the woman who died worked for the carnival. She was a fortune teller . . . a soothsayer," I added to avoid another lengthy definition.

"Perhaps she told a bad fortune," he suggested.

I laughed but then paused to think about it. "I hadn't really thought of that. Good point. But I think this whole murder might have more to do with betrayal and jealousy, a crime of passion, so to speak. It seems the victim was involved in an extramarital affair, and, as you well know"—I looked pointedly at him—"Those never turn out well. Of course, there was also a jilted lover in the mix, and Tad did say he saw Calvin hanging around Cherise's tent." I was talking out loud to myself now, ignoring my captive audience of one. "Then there was the murder weapon, which happened to be a tool Calvin might have used in his everyday maintenance schedule." I popped out of my musings and smiled up at Edward. "Thanks, this has been helpful. I've got to finish getting ready for work. And, Edward, try not to get so worked up about Ursula and Henry. Think of them more as entertainment than irritation."

"Small chance of that," he mumbled before vanishing.

CHAPTER 21

*M*yrna had music playing quietly on her computer as I walked in. She was humming and doing a dance on her chair as her fingers ran speedily over her keyboard. "Morning, Sunni," she said in a sing-song voice to match the music coming out of the computer.

"Morning, Myrna." Parker's office door was shut. There was no sign of Chase, which probably meant they were in a meeting. I wondered if Parker had gotten over his bad mood and momentary panic about eventually losing his job to the owner's future son-in-law. Parker's mood changed as much as the weather in spring, so I was counting on a much more congenial version this morning. I was anxious to talk to him to let him know that my carnival story had morphed into a murder story and that I was hot on the trail of all the good, juicy tidbits. I figured good, juicy tidbits sounded like something that would get people to pick up the paper. That was all Parker cared about anyhow, that people read the paper, which, in turn, kept the advertisers happy.

I sat at my desk and was just logging onto the computer when Parker's door opened. Chase walked out with a satisfied grin. It seemed his wealthy fiancée had bought him yet another sharp, expensive dress shirt, this one a pale blue with thin orange pinstripes. It had dawned on me that Rebecca Newsom liked to dress her betrothed. Admittedly, Chase was a handsome man with hazel eyes and striking features, although not nearly as striking as a certain detective. Rebecca enjoyed dressing Chase up to look like a model in a clothing catalogue, and Chase, who seemed somewhat obsessed about his appearance, didn't seem to mind playing the part.

"Morning, Sunni," Chase said as he headed to his desk.

"Morning," I said in return. We both worked in a small newsroom, doing the same job for the same paper and under the same editor, but we had never formed a bond. We were both two entirely different people, entirely different journalists.

"Taylor," Parker called from his office.

I hopped up ready to have our office chat and to fill him in on what I knew about the murder at the carnival.

"No need to meet this morning," Parker said. "I'm meeting with the printer. How is the carnival story going? Remember to make it sound glowing."

My mouth dropped open for a second before I realized and snapped it shut. "Uh, actually I wanted to talk to you about the carnival story. Obviously, after what happened yesterday, there's been a slight change in my storyline."

"Yeah, heard about the murder." He waved his thick hand Chase's direction. "Evans is going to cover the murder, so that leaves you free to skirt around the bad publicity and write a shining review."

"I was there when they discovered the body," I blurted. "I already have notes and interviews and details. It's only fair that I cover the murder." I hated to beg, especially with Chase sitting just a few feet away, but I was not beyond groveling this time. I'd already put too much time into it.

"That kind of story always goes to the lead reporter," Chase said smugly behind me. I didn't even bother to look at him because I already knew he was wearing a smug smile to go with it.

I got up from the desk to move closer to Parker. As far as I was concerned, this was a conversation I was having with the editor and not the lead reporter. "Parker, I spent the entire afternoon on this. I did interviews. I searched for evidence."

"She doesn't have to do any legwork," Chase interjected. "She just has to ask her boyfriend for the details. That's not journalism."

My face felt hot as I spun around. Chase and I normally just ignored each other, but I wasn't going to stand for this, even if he was marrying the owner's daughter. "For your information, Chase, all the evidence I gathered yesterday, I did on my own. My own 'legwork', unlike you. You'll head straight to the police department and wait around until someone is willing to fill you in on the details of the crime. That's hardly what I'd call legwork. Yes, I admit, I occasionally get access to things that most journalists don't because of my relat—" I cleared my throat. It was nobody's darn business. "Because of my friendship with Detective Jackson."

Chase's smooth dark brows danced a little, and his upper lip twitched. He hadn't expected me to fight back on this. "Well, I'm sorry that you spent so much time on this already, Sunni, but you had to know the assignment would fall on my desk. I cover the big stories. I'm sure your time isn't completely wasted. After all, you'll be writing about the carnival. Maybe I could see those notes," he suggested, without even an ounce of shame.

A million words built up in my throat, but before they could explode like a volcano, an eruption that would probably cost me my job, my unusually silent editor finally spoke up.

"Actually, Evans, I'm taking you off the assignment and giving it to Taylor. She was there when it happened. She's got all the insight and firsthand knowledge of the event. It would be wrong to let another reporter cover it."

It was Chase's turn for a red face. "Parker, are you sure about this?" he said with a clenched jaw. "I think you might be making a mistake."

Parker stood a little taller than usual. "Evans, I'm going to assume that you aren't threatening me because that would *truly* be a mistake." It seemed Parker had reflected on his worries yesterday and decided to stand up for his position by letting Chase know he was still in charge. If Newsom was planning on replacing Parker with Chase, he'd regret it. Something deep down told me Newsom was well aware of that. Chase was barely qualified to be a reporter, let alone the managing editor.

An awkward silence fell over the office. Myrna was sitting at her desk, watching and listening with such interest, I could almost imagine the bucket of popcorn sitting in front of her.

"Fine, let Sunni write the story about the murder. The mayor isn't going to be happy that the paper sensationalized bad press about his buddy Stockton's carnival." Chase said it with the same tone a kid might say 'go ahead and tell the teacher and see if I care'. He was trying to convince himself that he hadn't just lost a round with the boss.

"I'll deal with the mayor," Parker said directly to me. "Just get a good story."

"Thanks, Parker. I won't let you down."

CHAPTER 22

*A*fter my unexpected triumph in the newspaper office, I'd sat down to go through some of my notes, but I could feel Chase shooting flaming daggers at my back with his eyes. I grabbed my stuff and let Myrna know I was heading back to the carnival to further my investigation. I'd left with such speed, I really hadn't taken the time to plan my next move. I was still absorbing my victory, my first since I'd started working at *Junction Times*.

With the exception of the empty space, like a missing tooth, between the baseball throw and the ring toss, it was business as usual at the carnival. Day three had brought more teens without accompanying parents and less of the family units with little kids. That might have been because of the murder, or it might just have been the natural order of the spring fair business. Parents had probably already had their share of snow cones, sticky ride seats and long lines. Apparently, an unsolved murder wasn't enough of an impediment to put up a fight with an insistent teenager. As my mom used to say, there were few things less pleasant than a grumpy teen lazing about the house with nothing to do.

I stood in the spot where just yesterday the police and coroner were engaged in a flurry of activity. Today, the only sign that a tent had once sat in the spot was the dust free square in the middle of the pavement. That, too, would soon disappear as debris covered the clean asphalt.

"They came and took the tent away about an hour before we opened," the girl running the ring toss said. She handed two finger puppets, a cow and a pig, to the excited girl who had just won them. The winner shoved her new farm animal puppets on her fingers and hurried away with her friends.

The girl running the ring toss was customer free. I walked over to talk to her. She seemed surprised that her comment had earned her personal attention. She picked up the box with the finger puppets and quickly turned away from me to put the box on the shelf. I'd caught the name on her tag just before she spun away.

"Sarah, I'm a reporter with the *Junction Times*."

She turned back around and checked the pin on her nametag. "I know who you are. I saw you talking to Bri yesterday when we were all hanging out together trying to get over the shock of Cherise being—well, you know. Bri told us who you were after she rejoined the group. She said you were asking questions about Calvin. I hate to speak badly of Cherise, you know, now that she's gone, but Cal was too good for her. Cherise never treated him right. She was always putting him down in front of others and making fun of him."

"Sounds like it wasn't a great relationship," I said.

"Not that Cal would have, you know, well—" It seemed Sarah had an aversion to terms like murder, kill and dead. I couldn't really blame her. "He's got a temper, but basically, he's a good guy. This place couldn't run without him. At least the rides couldn't run, and without them, this carnival would be a joke." Unexpectedly, she reached out and grabbed my arm lightly. "But don't print that or Ivonne will fire me."

"Ivonne? Is Mrs. Stockton in charge of firing?" I asked lightly. "And don't worry. I won't print anything about our conversation."

"Phew, that's good to know. It's not that Carson doesn't fire someone occasionally. We had this guy Pete working for the carnival once. It turned out he was stealing a bunch of the food and selling it to another carnival at a nice, discount price. Carson gladly gave him the boot, but Ivonne is just a little meaner. It never seems to bother her to tell someone 'you're fired'. Whereas, I think Carson likes to avoid that kind of stuff."

"I see." I was slowly getting a much clearer picture of the various people on my suspect list. "Sarah, were you working yesterday when Cherise was discovered?"

"Yep, standing right here at the ring toss when Carson started yelling for help. Some guy was on his fifth try." She rolled her eyes. "Not a very good aim but I felt kind of bad because he was trying to impress his girlfriend."

"Did you notice anything suspicious before Carson called for help? Anyone hanging out around Cherise's tent or maybe someone arguing with her?"

Three teens came up to the booth and slapped down some money. Sarah paused our conversation to place the rings down in front of them. "To tell you the truth," she said to me, while she watched the rings get tossed. "We were pretty busy here yesterday, so I didn't really pay any attention."

"How about any of your coworkers? Were they hanging out around the tent when they should have been elsewhere?"

The first rings missed. Sarah handed them back to the kids for another try.

She walked closer to where I was standing. "I know Calvin was working on her generator earlier in the day, but he was supposed to be there. He's the person in charge of that kind of stuff. I saw Ivonne go into the tent at one point, but I think Cherise was with a customer because she came out pretty fast. I didn't see her after that."

"Woo hoo! You just won a prize," she cheered to her customers.

"Thanks for talking to me, Sarah. I'll let you get on with your work."

"Sure thing. I just hope they find the person soon. It's kind of, you know—" her eyes shifted quickly toward the ring throwers. She mouthed the word *scary* to me. Or at least that was my best guess.

"I'm sure they will. Thanks again."

CHAPTER 23

I wasn't sure what kind of reception I'd get from either Stockton, but I headed toward their RV. It was the same motorhome that Ivonne had stomped out of the day before red with anger about something, and the same place where I found Carson upset and no longer willing to sit for an interview.

The door was closed as I climbed the three steps. I peered through the rectangular window, a small one, but large enough to get a good view inside. The interior was dark except for the thin streams of light coming through two side windows. I peered through and caught movement on the right side of the space. Ivonne Stockton was standing next to Carson's desk ripping up some paper. She dropped it in the trash can next to the desk and then leaned over to churn around the papers and paper cups already in the can. It was easy to deduce that she was throwing away something and she didn't want anyone to see it.

Ivonne's expression was hard, and her mouth was pulled firmly from side to side. I spent a moment talking myself out of knocking. I was sure she wouldn't be pleased to see me. Then I remembered that I'd just pleaded for this assignment, and a vision of Chase, with his slicked back hair and expensive shirt, gloating and smirking, slipped through my mind. Without another second of hesitation, I lifted my hand and knocked confidently on the door.

Ivonne startled. She accidentally knocked over the can. Some of the contents spilled out. It was my opportunity. The door was unlocked. I opened it.

"I'm so sorry, Mrs. Stockton, I hadn't meant to startle you." I hurried toward her and stooped down. "Here, let me help you with that."

Ivonne waved me away. "No, please, there is sticky stuff and leftover food wrappers in here. My husband is always eating at his desk," she said with disgust. "I've got it." She quickly brushed all the debris into the can and set it upright. "What are you doing here? Surely, you can't expect us to take time out today for interviews?" Her tone had instantly grown snippy. "With circumstances the way they are," she added, "maybe it would be best to skip the article altogether. After all, we've been traveling here for the last twelve years. Everyone in town already knows all there is to know about the carnival."

That's because it never changes, I wanted to add but didn't. Naturally. "I'll have to let my editor decide that. I'm just the reporter."

"Then we'll just have to talk to your editor. I don't see how any article can put a positive light on this disastrous week in Firefly Junction." She shook her head and mumbled something about selling the whole darn outfit.

"I'm sorry?" I asked to clarify what she said.

"Not important. I've got to head out on site." She waved toward the door, letting me know it was time to go. She walked out behind me, shut the door and rushed past me once I was down the steps. I trailed behind slowly and waited for her to disappear into the activity.

I spun back around and climbed the steps. I hadn't noticed her make any effort to lock the door. I reached the top step and glanced around. With the carnival in full swing, no one was hanging around the employee trailers, except me.

My hand trembled a little as I reached for the door handle. This plan was sneakier and perhaps more illegal than most of my other plans, but I desperately wanted to see the paper Ivonne had gone out of her way to destroy and hide in the trash. It was in pieces and jumbled in with a good deal of other rubbish, but something told me it would be worth the risk and the effort.

The handle clicked. My conscience made me hesitate for just a second but then I reminded myself that I needed to get to the bottom of the murder or I'd have no story to write. I was only digging through trash. It wasn't as if I was going to steal or search through the Stockton's private things. After appeasing my conscience, I glanced around once more. The coast was clear, so I opened the door and slipped inside of the RV.

My heart was pounding so I wasted no time. I raced to the trash can and dumped it out on the ground. I had no choice except to touch the trash, which, just as Ivonne had complained, was filled with leftover garbage from food and drink. There were also various crumpled papers, the typical kind one might find in an office wastebasket, printer mishaps, notes started and not finished, lists of items needed. Fortunately, Carson seemed to have the habit of just balling his paper trash up before tossing it. Ivonne had ripped hers into six or seven strips. I began pulling the strips free of the other trash. The note was handwritten in ink, but this wasn't the time or place for me to put the puzzle together and decipher it. I jammed each piece into my pocket. My fingers were sticky from spilled drips of soda and candy wrappers.

The last two pieces, significant ones that seemed to be from the center of the note and contained a lot of writing, were stuck to a paper plate that, from all clues, including boysenberry syrup, grease stains and dusts of powdered sugar, once held a funnel cake. I carefully peeled each strip free, working hard not to rip them.

Footsteps sounded on the metal stairs leading to the trailer. I shoved the syrupy strips into my pockets with the others and stooped down to shove the trash back into the can.

The door opened. Carson's expression turned hard like marble. "What on earth are you doing in here? And why are you digging in the garbage? Boy, you reporters stop at nothing."

I finished scooping up the last bits of trash and set the can upright. "I apologize. I came in here hoping to get that interview you promised yesterday, and clumsy me—I tripped over the can." My heart was beating fast, but I managed to give what I thought was a perfectly reasonable response.

"I wonder what your boyfriend, Detective Jackson, will think if he hears you've been breaking and entering."

"The door was unlocked," I said calmly, deciding getting frantic was only going to hurt my case. "I believe breaking and entering requires some kind of actual *breaking*." My attempt at humor wasn't working. "Yes, you've caught me, Mr. Stockton." I held up my sticky hands. "You've caught me trying to do my job. I was told to write a glowing review of the Stockton Carnival, and I was hoping to get information straight from the person who knows every aspect of how this place runs. An article is always stronger if the source of the information is quality and trustworthy. So naturally, I came to you." Where humor had missed, flattery seemed to work.

His mouth bubbled as if he was trying to stick to his guns but he was feeling bad about berating me. "Yes, all right. I understand you are just trying to do your job, but you shouldn't have just walked into this trailer."

I nodded. "Agreed. And again, I apologize profusely." I was silently congratulating myself and breathing a sigh of relief for diffusing the situation. "If you have a few minutes—"

"I don't," he said abruptly. "As you well know, yesterday's calamity has me fending off all sorts of problems. Frankly, you aren't the first reporter I've dealt with today. But I can tell you, the reporters from the nearby city are far more cutthroat. They are ready to run with one of those horror stories about a murderer lurking in the shadows of the tents and rides. It's the last thing we need. I just don't have time to talk to you or any reporter." His face drooped into sadness. "You people have to understand that Cherise was like a family member. We need time to grieve and absorb the loss."

When a phrase started with *you people*, you people being journalists, it rarely ended with a kind, heartfelt sentiment. I was relieved. The man looked genuinely distressed and rightly so, or maybe even more so since it seemed Cherise might have been more than just a *family* member.

My journalist's instinct told me to dig a little deeper into his feelings. I was dying to ask how Mrs. Stockton was doing, just to see his reaction. Would he be stunned by the question? Would there be any indication that he worried his wife might have been the culprit? But I decided not to bring her up, considering she was standing in the same spot, just seconds earlier, chewing me out for nosing around. With any luck, I would not come up in any conversation between them, otherwise my innocent explanation of wandering into the trailer to look for Carson would be blown. Carson had casually threatened to let Jackson know that I was in his trailer, breaking and entering was how he'd phrased it. I didn't need a lecture from Jackson on staying out of trouble and away from the investigation. So I left Mrs. Stockton's reaction out of our chat. A chat, it seemed, that was coming to an abrupt end.

Carson stuck his arm forward to point out the exit door, in case I missed it. "Now, I've got a lot of work to do, Miss Taylor, so please, if you wouldn't mind—"

"Yes, of course. I'll head out to the carnival and try and capture the essence and ambience of the festivities in my words." I was piling it on, but I was suddenly extremely thankful that the whole scene had gone so smoothly.

If only I'd gotten in a few more prying questions.

CHAPTER 24

Ten minutes of strolling around the teenager packed carnival led me to the conclusion that the terms *essence* and *ambience* were better attributed to an expensive Italian restaurant or a posh French bakery. Unless, of course, overused cooking oil and greasy popcorn odors could be considered an essence. Then there was plenty of that floating around.

I headed back to the office with my sticky pocket of paper strips. With any luck, the discarded note would point me in the right direction. I was slowly running out of ideas for the next steps in my investigation.

Myrna had left for lunch, and Parker was in his office making calls. I thought I'd gotten lucky enough to avoid Chase for the rest of the day, but the second I sat behind my desk, the door swung open and Chase strolled in with a burger and soda.

There was no usual greeting as he swept past me and clunked down hard on his chair. It seemed he wanted me to know he was still angry. I was too busy to worry about his little tantrum. I only wished that he had eaten the burger at the restaurant so that I would have the office to myself when I pulled the sticky strips of paper from my pocket.

It was silly to fret about. I cleared a spot on my desk, pushing the stapler and my plastic apple filled with paperclips out to the corner. I pulled off my coat, dug into the pocket and carefully dragged out the strips of paper. There were seven in all, including the two that were dotted with boysenberry syrup and powdered sugar. Ivonne had ripped the paper lengthwise, the reason why it was so hard to read in strips. Horizontal would have left words and sentences intact. I started with the two edges and, without too much effort, was able to fill in the rest of the puzzle.

Chase, in the meantime, had somehow found a way to make eating a burger a noisy affair. Normally, the scent of grilled onions and ketchup would have made my mouth water, but the disgusting sounds he made while eating turned my stomach instead. He chomped loudly, smacked his lips and took long, angry sips of his soda. He even made sure to rattle the crisp paper wrapper and smack his cup down hard on the desk. The entire barrage of sound effects was enough to send my shoulders up around my ears. But I refused to let him know that his chomping and slurping were bothering me.

I ran a piece of tape across the top and bottom of the paper just to keep the slivers from twittering in the ruffle of air fluttering through the overhead vent.

My puzzle was complete. In the meantime, my office coworker had reached the bottom of his soda cup. It seemed he was determined to drink every drop of liquid the second it melted off the remaining ice. He followed one long, particularly discordant draw of his straw with a noise I could only describe as slurp-cious.

I pushed off my desk. The wheels on my chair spun around, dragging the seat with it. "Seriously, Chase, how can a man wearing a fifty dollar Ralph Lauren dress shirt make this much noise eating lunch? If I didn't already know you were back there,

I'd swear four hungry pigs were sitting at the back of the newsroom eating a trough full of mashed potatoes and gravy."

He shrugged and stared at me over his cup as he sucked loudly on the straw.

I spun back to my desk. I had no choice except to block him out.

Some of the blue ink had smeared from the grease and other moisture in the trash can, but I could still read it. There was no letterhead or logo or date, and there was no name, greeting or, for that matter, a closing. I silently read the note.

Consider this your final warning. I know what is going on and I won't stand for it. You will leave Carson alone or I'll make sure you leave this carnival for good. I'll make sure you never work again. I'm sure it would be easy enough to find another fortune teller to take your place. Someone with actual talent. You've been warned.

It wasn't difficult to figure out that the stern and threatening letter was meant for Cherise, since, as far as I knew, she was the carnival's only fortune teller. It was equally easy to deduce that Ivonne had written it. Aside from the fact that I witnessed her shredding the paper and hiding it in the trash, it mentioned Carson. That ruled him out as the author of the letter. Ivonne was the only other person with the authority to threaten someone with losing their job.

I read it over once more. This was a letter written by a very angry person.

"That's what passes for journalism, eh?" Chase asked. He was still sitting at his desk, but thankfully, he had finished lunch. "Looks like your source is a trash can. Good work, Taylor."

I peered back at him over my shoulder. "Any good reporter looks for evidence in unlikely places. And, tell me, Mr. Evans, are you ever going to get over this tantrum? Or am I stuck with you gobbling your lunch and lobbing snide remarks over my shoulder for the rest of the year?"

He picked up his phone and keys. "You don't have to listen to either. I'm out of here. I've got work to do, real work, not trash digging and taping shredded paper back together." He stood up as if ready to make a dramatic exit but curiosity got the best of him. He slowed as he passed my desk. His green eyes shifted sideways as he tried to read what I had in front of me.

I threw both my arms over the paper to cover it, like I was covering my math test to hide the answers.

I smiled up at him. "I guess we've both reverted back to high school antics this afternoon. Good luck with your *real* work."

Continuing with the high school act, he shrugged and muttered the obligatory 'whatever' before walking out the door.

I stared back at the letter and quickly tapped myself on the temple. There was something even more important about the letter than the words. The handwriting was fast, and it seemed the author, most likely Ivonne, was pressing down extra hard on the pen. But what stood out the most was her handwriting style. She wrote the small letter f in the same way most of us had learned to write it in grammar school. There was no fancy finish or long tail at the bottom. It put a wrench in my theory that Ivonne was the killer.

But it wasn't enough to kill it dead, so to speak.

CHAPTER 25

*A*fter piecing together a note that was somewhat incriminating, I decided to head back to the carnival. When Jackson and I visited the carnival on Sunday, before any murder and before I knew I was writing a story about it, he'd introduced me to both Carson and Ivonne Stockton. In fact, Carson had been joyfully stumbling out of Cherise's tent when we met. Ivonne had been at the cotton candy booth. The usual girl was out on maternity leave and Ivonne was apparently one of the few people who knew how to make cotton candy. Jackson had promised to buy me some, one of my favorites, and we'd found Ivonne standing in the booth surrounded by wisps of sweet cotton. It didn't take a scientist to know that she walked away from the task with sticky shoes . . . and sticky everything, for that matter. It could easily have been Ivonne's shoes that left the sticky substance on the rug beneath Cherise's table. But I was jumping to conclusions. I needed much more evidence to zero in on a solid suspect.

On my way to the carnival, I'd even toyed with the notion that Carson, himself, was the killer. It was entirely possible he'd set up the dramatic exit from the tent, calling for help, and looking properly distressed, just to throw the police off seeing him as a possible suspect. He was the first person in the tent after she was killed. Was it coincidence or was he angry at Cherise for putting a wedge in his marriage? It would hardly seem fair if he blamed her, but what if she had threatened to expose the affair to everyone, even to the papers to ruin his reputation? What if she was blackmailing him in some way? Ugh, my mind was going off into all kinds of tabloid style tangents. I needed to focus on what I had so far, and so far, that wasn't much.

The crowd was lighter than it had been in the morning. It was well after lunch, and chances were, the early visitors had run out of money for games, ride tickets and goodies. A late afternoon lull seemed predictable. I was sure once parents got off work for the day, the place would once again fill up with people.

I headed straight to the cotton candy booth. A woman with her hair tied up in a tight bun, to keep it out of the way of the floating sticky cotton, was leaned over the hot metal basin swirling a paper cone around to collect sky blue strands of sugar. I waited for her to finish the cone. There were no customers at the stand. It seemed she was trying to get ahead for the night. A wise decision considering each cone took a few minutes to make.

"I'll be right with you," she said without looking up from her task. Some of the blue had floated up and caught in her dark brown eyebrow. She absently swiped at the strand, which only made more sugar stick to her face. "Argh," she grumbled to herself.

"I suppose that is far less fun than it looks," I said cheerily. "It's the job I wanted when I was a little kid. I remember leaving a circus with my parents and emphatically stating that when I grew up I would either be the person who got to dress the little ponies in their feathers and bells or I would be in charge of whipping up the cotton candy."

She smiled at my story as she took one last swirl around the sugar machine to pick up the last strands. She shut off the noisy machine and dropped her newly formed puff of cotton candy into a plastic bag.

"I don't know why," I said, "but whenever I see those pillowy trees of cotton candy, I think of Dr. Seuss. It just seems that they'd fit right into one of his landscapes."

With her hands sticky from sugar, she used her forearm to wipe away the lingering strand of cotton on her brow. That only served to make it melt into a sticky blue mess. "Ugh," she groaned. "This is, by far, the worst job on the lot. I don't know why I ever let Ivonne train me on how to twirl sugar. Guess I thought it looked like fun," she added. "Woo, boy, rant over. What can I get you?" Her nametag said Ronnie.

I pulled out my press pass. "Actually, Ronnie, cute name by the way. I'm with the *Junction Times*. I'm just wandering around interviewing folks about their jobs here at the carnival."

Her lips rolled in. She seemed to be assessing whether or not talking to a reporter was a good thing. Two days ago, before Cherise was murdered, she probably wouldn't have given it a second thought.

She chose the diplomatic way out. "I don't know much about what happened. I was off duty that afternoon."

"Oh, you're talking about the murder," I said, pretending as if it hadn't even crossed my mind. "I'm actually just doing interviews to write a general interest story about the spring fair and its yearly carnival." I reached across and pulled a feathery string of blue cotton off her shoulder. "I suppose this job is much harder and stickier than it looks. I was actually here on Sunday, and I had some cotton candy. Ivonne was making it, standing right where you are, with the same amount of loose candy threads clinging to her clothes and skin. She didn't look too happy about it either. When did she hand the reins over to you?" I hoped my personalized introduction would make my question seem offhand and not prying. I wanted to get an idea of what Ivonne was up to on Monday afternoon. If she was still running the cotton candy booth, then that would pretty much wipe her off the suspect list.

"I volunteered on Sunday, hoping to get in good with the boss. But now I see why there were no other volunteers. I've been at this on my own since Monday morning. I'm getting much better at it now. My first few tries were pretty pathetic, like weepy little willow trees of spun sugar." She giggled.

"Wow, so one day of training and then Ivonne set you free to be on your own. Did she at least check in with you on Monday? To make sure you weren't overwhelmed with stickiness?" I added my own giggle.

"Nah, Ivonne is always so busy. She helped me fill the machine on Monday morning and that was the last I saw of her. Probably a good thing."

It was an odd thing to say. "Oh? Why is that?" I asked, with a bit too much enthusiasm. I was hoping Ronnie had some insight into Ivonne's mood that day. I'd sure come across an angry version of her in the morning. I wondered if she had held onto that rage for the rest of the day.

"No reason really," she said. "I just would have hated for Ivonne to see what a terrible job I did with the first batch. Even the customers looked unhappy."

"Ah, I see." This time it was disappointment and not enthusiasm in my tone. "I'm sure the customers still enjoyed them. After all, sugar is sugar."

"True. Well, I'm going to spin some more cotton, if you don't mind." Ronnie flicked on the switch and the noisy machine fired up. "It's going to take me a week to get all of this sticky stuff off my skin and out of my hair, but it beats trying to get the smell of barbecue beef and chicken out of it. I was working the barbecue booth at the last carnival and it was not fun."

"Then maybe volunteering to learn the art of cotton candy

making wasn't such a bad choice after all. Thanks for talking to me." I stepped back.

"Watch it," Ronnie jutted her arm forward and pointed with a paper cone.

I froze in my spot and looked back over my shoulder to see that I'd nearly backed into a man pushing a large handcart that was loaded with overflowing trash cans. I stepped forward to clear the way for him. As he rolled the cans past, I inadvertently spotted what looked to be fabric, instead of the usual clutter of used paper and plastic. I couldn't tell for certain, but it looked like the sleeve end of a gray sweatshirt. Why would someone throw away a sweatshirt?

CHAPTER 26

$\mathcal{I}$ followed casually along behind the man and his handcart laden with trash cans. It seemed certain that he was hauling his heavy load to the back of the lot where the portable toilets were lined up in front of a long trash bin that had been brought in for the carnival. The man was younger, maybe twenty-five, and he was wearing the same green striped shirt that Calvin wore. It seemed to be the uniform for the maintenance crew.

He hadn't noticed the silly woman tagging along behind him to the trash until he parked the handcart next to the long bin.

"Excuse me," I said.

I hadn't seen his earbuds until he pulled them out. He tucked them into his pocket next to his phone and pulled out a pair of latex gloves. "The porta potties are right there," he said, assuming that would be the only reason for me to be milling about the area.

"Yes, I see them." I crinkled my nose. "They are hard to miss. Actually, I know this sounds crazy but where did these cans come from?"

Lance, as his nametag stated, had sunglasses hanging on the top of his shirt. He put them on. "They're from the ride area." He pointed to the one where I saw the sweatshirt sleeve. "This one was behind the Lovers' Lane ride, and this one was from the Ferris wheel. Did ya lose something?"

"Yes, that's it," I said too abruptly. "Yes. I lost something. This is silly but I was tossing my cup out in the can next to the Lovers' Lane ride, and I accidentally tossed my car keys into it. At least, I think that's what happened. I was holding them one minute, and the next, they were gone."

Lance shrugged. "I usually just dump them into the bin. If you want to dig through the trash, go ahead. Are you sure this is the one you want to see?" He pointed to the one with the sweatshirt.

"Yes, you said that's the one that came from outside the Lovers' Lane ride, right?" Of course, the location of the can didn't matter too much, but it gave more credibility to my story.

"Yep."

"Then that's the right can."

He was nice enough to remove the can from the handcart and place it on the ground so I could rummage through it, something I didn't relish doing, but I had to make it look good.

"Lance, right?" I asked pointing to his nametag.

"Yeah, that's right."

"You've been so nice, I hate to ask but you don't happen to have another pair of those latex gloves?"

"I might." He reached into the pocket of his pants and fished out another pair of gloves. "They haven't been used." He handed me them.

"Thanks so much. You've been a great help." I pulled the gloves on as he set to work lifting and dumping the other can. What a glamorous life I led. It seemed I would once again be digging in trash.

I gingerly moved things around, pretending to be searching for keys, while actually just working to pull free the gray fabric. My first guess had been right. It was a gray sweatshirt that had been jammed into the trash can. I pushed away some of the debris, popcorn buckets, half eaten hot dogs and empty soda cups to free the sweatshirt. It was covered in stains, which wasn't surprising considering it had been inside a pile of trash. I yanked on the garment and pulled it halfway free. There were stains on the sleeve and front panel along the zipper. Some were purplish stains from a soda or snow cone. A few stains were greasy but a dark substance was splattered over the entire right sleeve and a good portion of the right panel. I was no forensic expert but it didn't look like a food substance. It looked like blood. I scraped at one of the bigger stains. The rust red color that came off on my glove sent a chill through me. Someone had thrown the sweatshirt away because it was covered in blood.

"Any luck?" Lance asked, yanking me from my stunned thoughts.

I looked up. "No luck. I'm starting to wonder if I left them on a ride or at a food booth."

"You could check at the entrance. They keep a box filled with lost and found items." His eyes fell to the sweatshirt I was still holding in my hand.

"People throw away the craziest stuff, don't they?" he said. "Looks like it was a perfectly good sweatshirt and now it's ruined."

I pushed it back into the debris, not wanting him to take a closer look. "Yes, someone must have decided it was too hot, and they didn't want the burden of carrying around a sweatshirt."

I pulled the gloves off and dropped them into the can. "I really appreciate your help, and I'll stop at the lost and found. I'm sure that's where I'll find my keys." I looked at the massive bin. I'd seen similar ones at construction sites where something was being torn down or dismantled. "I guess you'll need to throw this can into the bin too."

"Yeah, if you're through with it," he said. As he spoke, he pulled what appeared to be a crinkled to-do list out of his pocket.

"It's just that I'd kind of like to make sure I find the keys first. Is there any way you could leave this one can right here and toss it out later tonight?" I planned on letting the police know about the trash can. It would be much easier for them if they didn't have to rummage through an entire bin.

He unfolded the paper and mumbled the phrase 'sanitize water faucets'. He shoved the paper back into his pocket. "Yeah, I've got an extra can to replace it."

"That would be great, Lance. By the way, how often do these cans get emptied?"

"Depends on where they sit in the carnival. If a can is sitting right next to the barbecue stand, a popular food place where everyone uses a mountain of napkins, the can has to be dumped twice a day. But since this can sits far back from the main pathway between the rides, it only gets dumped every three or four days."

"So I was just digging through three days of trash," I said with a laugh. "Yuck. I hope I won't have to come back to it and dig farther."

Lance put the emptied can back on his handcart and left the filled one next to the bin. I walked along with him, hoping to get a few more nuggets of information.

"I noticed you're wearing the same green striped shirt as Calvin. Is that what all the maintenance people wear?"

"Yeah. Calvin is my boss. How do you know him?"

"We met on Monday. I work for the *Junction Times*, and Carson had me shadow Calvin for the safety check so I could write about it in the paper." We picked up our pace as we passed the portable bathrooms. "Calvin wasn't too happy to have me tagging along but I learned a lot."

"Can't imagine why anyone would want to read about that boring stuff in the paper," Lance said.

"I see your boss writes you a to-do list," I said airily. "Mine does too. It's kind of annoying, and my boss has such sloppy writing that I can barely read it."

"Yeah, Cal never won any penmanship award, that's for sure."

I had to walk faster to keep up with his long stride. "Do you mind if I look at your to-do list? I just want to see if it's as sloppy and hard to read as the one I get." It was a lame excuse, but it was the best I could do on short notice. Finding the sweatshirt was quite possibly game changing, but I hardly expected the chance to check out Calvin's writing too. It seemed I'd hit the jackpot twice. Lance stopped the cart and pulled out the list. He unfolded it.

"It's a little worse because he's been kind of out of it," he said.

I took hold of the crumpled list and smoothed it between my fingers just to make sure. The word faucets was written with a plain, old grammar school f. I smiled. "Yep, looks like you have to deal with the same handwriting mess as me." I handed the paper back to him.

Lance pushed the paper into his pocket and paused to take his earbuds out. I had to work quick before I lost him to his own world of music.

"How is Calvin doing?" I asked. "I heard he was close with Cherise, the poor woman who died yesterday."

I sensed he wasn't expecting me to bring up Calvin's feelings or the murder. "He's all right, I guess. Besides, they weren't close anymore. Cherise was always treating him like dirt, like he didn't have feelings or something. He's been much easier to work for since they broke up. She was always putting him in a bad mood, then he'd take it out on the rest of us."

"Oh, that's too bad. Well, I'll let you get back to your music. Thanks for leaving the can there for now."

"Hope you find your keys."

CHAPTER 27

I hurried back through the most crowded areas of the carnival to a peripheral place with benches where an elderly woman sat with a baby stroller and a young dad sat with a sleeping toddler on his lap. It was a sort of out of the way rest place for people waiting for other family members to finish their rides or games. I found my own space alone at the end of a bench and pulled out my phone. With any luck, I'd catch Jackson with a free second to answer his phone.

"Hey, Bluebird, what's up?" his deep voice always sent a little thrill through me.

"Well, as you can probably guess by the background noise, I'm at the carnival."

"Are you?" he said with a touch of suspicion. "And, of course you're staying clear of killers and murder investigations."

"Now, you know me better than that, Detective Jackson." A woman sat down on the same bench, so I got up and moved out of hearing range of the others. I lowered my voice just in case. "Has Officer Reed found anything of significance?" I asked, hoping to squeeze any details out of him that I could.

"I haven't talked to her. Since I'm not on the case, it's not really my place to ask. And since you're not on the case—" he started.

"Well, her team might have missed the proverbial smoking gun," I blurted quickly to halt the forthcoming admonishment.

Music strummed through the phone. "Where are you at?" I asked.

"I'm chasing bad guys. Or at least hoping to chase them. I'm at a mall tracking down the seller of those flashing light shoes. Back to your little bombshell. What smoking gun?"

"I realize I'm not a professional investigator—" I said with enough sarcasm that it practically dripped off my phone, "however, I think the evidence team might have missed a big clue. The maintenance man was pushing several trash cans to the big bin at the rear of the carnival grounds. I happened to notice the sleeve of a gray sweatshirt sticking up through the pile of expected carnival rubbish. Thinking it was strange, I followed the man and made up an excuse that I was looking for lost keys. It took some doing but I pulled a good portion of the sweatshirt free. Guess what was splattered all over it?"

"I'm guessing it wasn't blue cherry snow cone," he said.

"Nope, it was blood. Or at least that is my unprofessional opinion."

I sensed that he had stopped walking. "Were you wearing gloves?"

"Of course. I borrowed some from the maintenance guy."

"Where is the sweatshirt now?" he asked.

"I left it in the can. Far be it from me to intrude on a police investigation."

He had a good laugh over my last remark. "Could be someone had a bloody nose or some other mishap, but I'll call Reed so she can get over there to take it in for analysis."

"Lucky for Officer Reed I had the wherewithal to find out what location the can had come from. It was the trash can next to the Lovers' Lane ride, and because that particular can isn't in a busy traffic area, the maintenance guy said it only gets dumped every three or four days. So the sweatshirt could easily have been in the can since Monday."

"Good work on that, Sunni. I mean it. I'll call Officer Reed right now. What are you up to next? Or should I ask?"

"I'll probably mill about the carnival a little bit longer. I have an article to write, and it's got to be a zinger because I really stuck my neck out this morning."

"Gee, that's so not like you," his sarcasm was equally drippy.

"Yes, well, at the newspaper office I decided I'd surrendered a good story to Chase just once too often. Because of the murder, Parker switched him to the carnival story, but I stood my ground and there might have even been a little foot stomping while I stood it. Much to my delight and to Chase's chagrin, Parker landed on my side for once. I think he's tired of constantly having to acquiesce and grovel to the owner's future son-in-law."

Jackson paused. I thought the call had dropped until his rich, deep voice floated through the phone again. "You know what I love about you, Bluebird?" he asked.

My face warmed as I held the phone against my ear. "My sparkling smile?"

"Well, that, of course."

"My can do attitude?" I tried again.

"Yes, that too. Except sometimes I wish you had a little less of that when it came to tracking down killers. I love that you can use chagrin, acquiesce and grovel in the same thought and make it sound perfectly normal. I'll have to pull out my old SAT study guide to look two of those up, but I love the way you talk and think. There's more on that list but I'm standing in the middle of a crowded mall and someone might hear. Good for you, Sunni. I'm glad Parker wised up and handed you the assignment. Now, speaking of assignments, I need to track down the source for those shoes before those two bozos knock over another bank . . . or worse, hurt or kill someone in the process."

"Go get 'em," I cheered. "And don't forget to tell Officer Reed."

"Right, I'll do that now. Maybe we can meet later."

"Sounds good." I hung up and headed back into the carnival.

I decided I deserved a sweet reward for finding the sweatshirt, even if it didn't turn out to be evidence. A syrup drenched funnel cake was calling my name.

I weaved through the crowd and made my way toward the long line at the funnel cake stand when Queen Melinda's trio of friends caught my eye. I realized, then, that I hadn't seen the queen and her entourage once this afternoon. Maybe her royal duties were finished. The chattier friend, with the stylish bob haircut, noticed me heading toward the funnel cakes and waved. Since we were obviously on friendly terms, I took it as my cue to ask some questions.

I reached the girls and noticed that they were all stretching up tall to look past me. "Are you here with Detective Jackson?" one of them asked.

"No, he's working." Apparently, I was being used to catch a glimpse of Detective Jackson. That certainly didn't help my self-esteem. "Where is the queen?" I asked, forging ahead right past their disappointed frowns.

The second friend, who I had pinned as the more talkative one, chimed in. "She wasn't feeling well this morning. I think she's still upset about—"

Her friend elbowed her discretely to stop her midsentence.

"She's just upset about what happened to that poor woman in the fortune telling tent," the girl continued. "She'll be here later to hand out free balloons."

"That's nice. Well, I'm off to buy a funnel cake. Have fun."

"You too," the first girl said. "And you should bring Detective Jackson to the carnival later. I hear the Lovers' Lane ride is lots of fun." She winked at me as if were best buddies.

"Thanks for the suggestion." I waved lightly and returned to my funnel cake mission.

CHAPTER 28

The funnel cake had spoiled any thoughts of a reasonable dinner. Ursula and Henry had packed up and cleared out for the night. Ever since the incident at Christmas, when Edward lost his ghostly temper and yanked the hammer out of Ursula's hand, she had rushed to get out of the house before dark. I was all right with that. I almost always saw them before work, particularly when they were helping themselves to my coffee and whatever leftovers I had in the fridge, so it was nice to come home to an empty house. Well, technically empty, if I didn't count dogs and ghosts.

I parked the jeep and walked out to the road, to the mailbox. I sorted through the bills and advertisements and found an envelope that had been addressed personally, by a rather shaky hand. Cider Ridge Inn was written on the line below my name. According to the return address, it was from Henrietta Suffolk, the elderly woman who was a descendant of Cleveland Ross's cousins. After the tragic duel and the discovery that Bonnie Ross was carrying Edward's child, Cleveland sent her away in disgrace. He was kind enough to make sure she was taken care of by distant relatives. I had been determined to uncover the details about Edward's child because I was sure that was why Edward had been stuck in limbo, destined to spend eternity floating through the walls of the inn. But now I wasn't so sure. His mood seemed to darken and his ghostly emotions seemed to intensify with each revelation.

I pulled the thick envelope out from the pile of mostly junk mail. I'd discovered that Bonnie had taken back her maiden name, Milton, and her son, Edward's son, had been named James Henry Milton. He was born in 1817 but that was all I knew about him. It seemed I was about to learn more. I'd take the letter to my room, a place that Edward's gentlemanly sensibilities would not allow him to enter. That way I could read it without him peering over my shoulder. Then I'd decide whether or not to relay the news to Edward.

My impatient dogs had not waited for me to reach the front door. They'd dashed through the dog door in the kitchen and raced around to the front yard to greet me. Newman immediately dropped a tennis ball at my feet.

"It's getting too dark," I told the insistent dog. He crouched down on his haunches, swung his tail like a helicopter blade and stared at the ball with laser focus. I picked it up and threw it across the front yard. He plowed through the grass and weeds and retrieved it before it hit the ground. He came prancing back ready for more, until I said the magic word.

"Cookie?"

Now I had Redford's attention too. The three of us walked inside, then they trotted ahead to the kitchen, in case I'd forgotten where the *cookies* were kept. I placed the pile of mail on the desk I used to write lists and notes and carried the letter from Henrietta Suffolk to my bedroom. I was anxious to see what she had written, but I knew the dogs were even more anxious for the promised treat.

I walked back out to the kitchen and straight into the pantry for the dog cookie jar. I tossed out two bone shaped goodies and shut the pantry door.

"Why were you making a point of hiding that letter?" Edward's voice rarely startled me anymore, even when it rolled out long before his image, but this time I jumped. Only because he had caught me doing exactly what he'd accused me of.

"I wasn't hiding it. I just wanted to read it in private."

"Well, I'm certain that—your suitor," he said before something stupider came out, "has never handwritten a letter in his life, so I can only assume it's from someone else, the woman who claims to know all about Bonnie and my child."

"She claims—actually, claimed, to know nothing of the sort."

"Why claimed?"

"Henrietta Suffolk died recently. She was ninety-five."

"Good lord, who lives to ninety-five?"

"Lots of people do these days."

He made a full appearance instead of the wavering half image that had startled me in the first place. "It's a wonder people these days live that long when they spend so much time sitting and staring at tablets and driving those machines to and fro. And some of the foods I've seen you eat—"

"How did this become a discussion on my eating habits?" I pulled the milk out of the refrigerator. "Which, other than the fact that I just downed a funnel cake piled high with syrup and sugar, are perfectly reasonable and healthy. Sometimes. And, medical science has become quite advanced since your time. Your gunshot wound would have been easily fixed today. You probably wouldn't have spent more than a few days in a hospital bed, then you would have been up and about annoying people."

"Then, it seems I died in the wrong era. Perhaps that's why I'm lingering in this world."

"I hardly see how that would help you now. It's not as if the doctors can fix you all up and send you right back into humanity."

I sat at the table with my glass of milk, happy to give my feet some rest after long hours at the carnival.

"Someone is particularly brash this evening," he drifted toward the table.

"Sorry, guess I'm on a sugar high from the funnel cake."

"I don't know what this is, this funnel cake, but you should probably avoid eating another one."

"No argument here." I sipped the milk.

Newman, now finished with his treat, realized his favorite incorporeal being was in the room. He snatched his tennis ball off his pillow and trotted over to where Edward was *leaning* against the counter. "You ridiculous animal, I've already thrown that ball a dozen times today." He swept the ball up in his transparent hand and tossed it out into the hallway. Newman chased after it.

"Why are you hiding Miss Suffolk's letter? Are you afraid the information she's sent you will push me into some kind of fit?"

I leaned back and marveled for a second at how well the man could read me. "Not a fit," I said, "but the ghostly version of depression. I guess they would have called it melancholy or low spirits in your day."

"There's hardly a chance of that. I never get low spirits. My moods are as flat and smooth as a lake on a breezeless day."

A laugh shot from my mouth before I could stop it. Or maybe I had no intention of stopping it. "You mean your moods are as flat and smooth as the ocean during a raging tempest."

Newman returned with the ball and dropped it right through Edward's Hessian boot. Edward blew at it. There was just enough anger behind his breath that the ball shot like a bullet into the hallway again.

I peered up at him. "I believe you just made my case. Frankly, Edward, I'm not certain you're ready for any of this."

"Any of what? Playing fetch with a silly dog?"

"Funny. You know what I'm talking about. Maybe it's better if you don't know. At least for now."

He drifted back toward his favorite place on the hearth. It was the place he sat when he was thinking, and I could tell by the wavering, semi-invisible image drifting across the kitchen he was deep in thought.

I waited for him to settle and reappear. "I'll admit, I had considered not knowing anything about my son. As you've mentioned, he could have died young or lived through some other tragedy. Or worse—he could have been poor, a beggar in the streets." Quite often the snooty, shallow side of Edward Beckett made an appearance.

"Are you saying you would prefer to learn that James died young of some malady rather than hear that he was poor?"

"Not a malady, certainly. Beckett's don't die from something as mundane as a malady. A fall from a great steed perhaps or—" He paused to contemplate. I decided to fill in the blank.

"Or from a duel after he scandalously sullied another man's wife, the man who was kind enough to put a roof over the head of the man who would have otherwise been penniless and poor?"

"Well, you've certainly put me in my place, haven't you?" Instead of his facial features sharpening, something that happened when he was angry, they faded and became distorted, his usual reaction when he was upset. I bit my lip, something *I* did when I wanted to take back my words.

"I'm sorry, Edward, that was uncalled for. Maybe we should just drop the subject. It always gets unpleasant when we start talking about this. I'll understand completely if you don't want to know anything else about James Henry Milton."

He swept past me to the window, a cool rush of air followed him. "Must you keep saying his name? And it's not Milton. If I had —If I had been alive when he was born, I would have insisted his name be Beckett." He gazed out the window into the darkness.

I watched him for a moment as he stared out with a faraway look that I'd caught more than once. I walked over to him. "Then you do care about what happened to your baby?"

"Of course, I do. I might occasionally sound pompous and callous, a result of my upbringing, I'm afraid, but there is—or was, a genuine heart once beating in this chest."

We were in the midst of one of those moments when I wished he were flesh and blood so I could put a kind hand on his shoulder or even hug him. But Edward would never experience either again, and that saddened me. But certainly, since I'd managed to hurt his feelings with my words, I could give comfort as well.

"I'd like to think that if we were both born in the same era, that you and I would have been good friends. I think we would have gotten along."

My words seemed to help. He nodded faintly. "Perhaps even lovers."

"Well, I gave it my best shot," I said. "As usual, you blew up our moment." I headed toward my bedroom

"I'd like to know." His voice followed me down the short hallway to my room.

I stopped and turned back. He was still at the window, but he was looking toward me. "I know when you hide yourself in your bedroom, your little sanctuary away from your irritating house spirit, you'll be reading about my son. I'd like to hear about him." He paused. "No matter what you find."

"All right." I spun back around but ended up making a full circle to face toward him again. "My little sanctuary," I repeated his words. "Cherise must have had a little sanctuary, a place away from the bustle of the carnival. Why didn't I think of this before? Thank you, for that, Edward."

"I have no idea what your are blathering on about, but you're welcome."

CHAPTER 29

I rushed back out of the house, leaving the letter from
Henrietta Suffolk unopened for now. I had a case to
solve. Only my brilliant plan and the enthusiasm for my next
endeavor was dampened by the prospect that I would face obsta-
cles trying to get into Cherise's personal things. I knew there were
at least half a dozen motorhomes and fifth wheels parked in the
RV area of the park near the carnival. I knew the first one
belonged to the Stocktons, but which one, if any, did Cherise bunk
in? In my first conversation with Carson Stockton, over the telephone, before all of the critical events, he'd given me a quick
summary of the ins and outs of owning a traveling carnival.
Employee turnover for his carnival was particularly low, he had
boasted, mostly because they provided free living quarters for the
workers during their travels. He'd mentioned that some of his
competitors made their employees 'fend for themselves' when it
came to room and board. He also mentioned that a few of his
employees opted to rent nearby motel rooms instead of sharing a
motorhome with workmates but that most of them took advantage of the free bed. I hoped Cherise was one of those people.

I was still chiding myself for not thinking of the plan sooner but then I came to the conclusion that I'd sort of considered Madame Cherise's tent as her home away from home. It might have been because Raine lived in the same house where she ran her psychic business but that was, of course, silly because Raine lived in a little house in town, not in pop-up tent.

As I'd predicted, after the late afternoon lull, the crowds had returned for the evening festivities. The weather had improved with a navy blue night sky and just a nip of chill in the air. People were clad in light jackets and the occasional beanie or hat to cover ears, but the jovial conversations and laughter made it clear spring break was in the air.

My plan was to head to the kiddie rides where Brianna worked. It felt as if we'd formed a bit of a bond. I considered her my best source for information only the employees would know.

My phone rang as I climbed out of the jeep. It was Jackson.

"You'll never guess where I am again," I said.

"I don't need to guess. I can hear the horn tooting music of the carnival through the phone. I thought you spent the day there."

"I did but I had a few things to check out."

"Why does that sound like something I'm against," he said.

"It's perfectly safe and no big deal at all. I promise I won't be climbing onto any horse carriages. Are you still at the mall? Did you track down the shoe seller?"

"As a matter of fact I did, and the shoe seller had a description of the customer that fit with the ones given by the robbery witnesses, at least the bits of details they could see beneath the sweatshirt hoods, bandana scarves and dark sunglasses. Unfortunately, but not surprisingly, the customer paid with cash, so there was no financial lead to follow. I've got some news you'll be interested to hear though. It's about your smoking gun. Turned out you had something there."

I stopped outside of the carnival and scooted away from the

noise. "Did I? How exciting. Can you tell me since I was the source of the evidence? Please. Pretty please?"

"What kind of a meanie do you take me for, Bluebird? I wouldn't have told you just to tease you. It turned out that the blood on the sweatshirt belonged to Cherise. The splatter marks indicate that the killer was wearing it when he brought the heavy bar down on Cherise's head."

"He?" I asked anxiously. "You said he? Do they have a suspect? Did I lead them to the suspect?" It wouldn't have been as exciting as actually narrowing it down myself, but it was good to know I had a hand in it all.

"It just so happened that they found an employee nametag in the pocket. The pin on the back was broken. He must have jammed it in the pocket and then forgotten all about it when he ditched the sweatshirt . . . allegedly, anyhow."

"I'm going to assume you're not telling me this and teasing me with the pronoun *he* just because you're in an ornery mood."

"If I tell you, you have to promise that you're not going to walk into that carnival and head straight to the Lovers' Lane ride to confront the guy."

"Why would I do that? Jeez, one little thrill ride in a horse carriage and you treat me as if my head is filled with cotton candy."

"A thrill ride? Is that what we're calling it now?"

"Enough of that. I promise I won't confront the guy. Is it Calvin, the maintenance man? I knew he had a hand in it. Cherise broke his heart—"

"The guy's name is Cody. They might have already pulled him in for questioning."

"Cody? Huh, seems like I've heard that name before. So this case might be solved."

"No arrest yet," he said, "but the sweatshirt is a darn good piece of evidence. Thanks to you."

I couldn't help but smile. "Yep, thanks to me."

"They unlocked Cherise's phone too," he continued. "There were plenty of texts from someone who she had nicknamed Sweetie. It turned out to be Carson's number, and from the content, it was obvious they were more than boss and employee."

"I guess that's no surprise to either of us. Anything else on the phone?"

"Not that I know of. Enough shop talk, I'm hungry." Jackson said. "I've got a hankering for a hot dog with the works. I can meet you at the carnival."

"Sure. Just text me when you get here, and I'll meet you at the entrance."

"All right, should be about twenty minutes. See you soon." He hung up.

As far as I was concerned, if there was no arrest, then the case wasn't solved yet. There had to be more evidence. Twenty minutes didn't give me a lot of time. I was sure Jackson wouldn't love the idea that I was trying to get into the employee trailers to snoop around in Cherise's belongings. I needed to finish the search before his text.

I wasted no time heading toward the area of carnival that was roped off as the little kid section with the teeny train ride and the airplanes and cars that went round and round on a circular track. I wasn't three steps into the kid zone when I remembered where I'd heard the name Cody. Brianna's boyfriend, Cody, who did double duty as a truck driver and as the operator of the Lovers' Lane ride. What motive could he have had to kill Cherise? Was he seeing Cherise too? Brianna certainly didn't mention any connection with her boyfriend when she talked about Cherise.

The latest revelation hit me like a bag of bricks. It also derailed my plan to talk to Brianna. Another girl was running the airplane ride. Brianna was either off for the night or so shaken that Cody had been taken in for questioning, she couldn't work. I decided it wouldn't hurt to ask the girl running the airplane ride.

I waited for her to walk around to each little airplane to make sure the teeny pilots were belted in. She got back to the control panel and did a cute little announcement telling the pilots the runway was clear for takeoff. Giggles and yells squirted through the night air as the airplanes stuttered forward and then lifted a few feet off the ground.

"Hello, I know you're busy, but I was looking for Brianna. She mentioned that she was going to be working the airplane ride."

The girl had rainbow framed glasses and two silver peace signs hanging from her ears. "Are you a friend?" she asked.

"Just an acquaintance."

"Are you with the police? Brianna's not here," she continued, without my answer. It seemed police or not, she didn't want to get involved. "She took the night off."

"I see. Is she in her trailer? I'm not with the police. I was just hoping to talk to her."

"Yeah, I think she took some aspirin. She'd been crying a lot." She drew her lips tight as if she worried she'd said too much.

"Poor thing. She's in the third RV from the end, right?" I asked, deciding to just throw a guess out there.

"Fourth." She turned back to the control panels to focus on her little pilots.

"Thanks." I walked quickly toward the back of the lot where the motorhomes were parked. I wasn't sure exactly how to go about my next plan, but I was sure something would come to me when I got there.

I'd used up about five minutes of my precious time just walking from one end of the carnival to the other and back again. A light was on in the fourth motorhome. I had no time to come up with any elaborate ruse or explanation as to why I was lurking around the trailers. I marched toward the vehicle, then a thought stopped me short. During our last conversation, Brianna had pointed out Cody. He was stooped forward with hands in his pockets, seemingly trying to avoid the frigid air coming down off the mountains. I'd mentioned that he looked cold. She told me that someone had taken his sweatshirt while he was working. I should have thought of it before. I blamed it on the emotional kerfuffle I was dealing with at home with Edward.

I walked up the three steps and knocked.

"Who is it?" a wavering voice called through a small open window on the side of the RV.

"Uh, is that you, Brianna? It's Sunni Taylor from *Junction Times*. We met a few days ago."

I expected a 'go away, I don't want to talk to anyone' response but was surprised when the door opened. Brianna's nose was red and her eyes were puffy. She was clutching a pillow with the names Cody and Brianna stitched into it.

"What are you doing here?" she asked with a sniffle.

"It's sort of complicated." I decided to go with a straightforward approach. As much as I would have liked to start with a few minutes of comforting words, I had no time to waste. I needed to get straight to it. "My real job is a reporter, as you know, but I'm also a part-time private investigator of sorts. I don't get paid for it, of course, but I dabble in solving local murders." So much for getting straight to it. I was, as Edward would be keen to point out, blathering on. "Brianna, I heard about Cody and I'm very sorry."

"He didn't do it." She pushed the pillow over her face to stifle a sob, then lowered it. "Cody hardly even knew Cherise. I don't think they ever spoke. Some of the girls were whispering that they were seeing each other and that was why she broke it off with Calvin. But they are wrong. Cody loves me." She hugged the pillow tightly against her and a loud hiccough followed. "Darn, there I go again with those stupid hiccoughs."

"Let's get you a drink of water," I said. "If you don't mind me coming in for a second, I want to talk to you about the murder. If Cody had no motive and he hardly knew Cherise, then the police will soon discover that they have the wrong person. And I can attest to the fact that you told me his sweatshirt was stolen while he was working."

Her mouth dropped open and she blinked her puffy eyes in surprise. "How did you know about the sweatshirt?"

I'd stumbled and needed to recover quickly. I couldn't let her know that I'd caused this terrible chain of events for Cody. "I have a connection at the police station. Since I'm covering the carnival, my friend keeps me caught up on the investigation."

With her red nose and puffy eyes, she reminded me of a little girl who had lost her kitten. "Did you tell your friend that Cody lost his sweatshirt?" she asked weakly.

"I didn't at the time because, to be honest, I only just now remembered. But I promise, I will tell him first chance I get."

Brianna stepped back to silently invite me inside. It was a cramped space that reminded me of a large storage container. It was crammed full of six mattresses each partnered with a short, narrow chest of drawers and a lamp. The kitchenette in the center was no more than a sink and two cupboards with a built in microwave. A dorm room sized refrigerator was jammed under the counter. A few of the personal spaces were decorated with posters and family pictures, but it was hardly inviting or homey. Life on the road certainly afforded no luxuries.

"The police have the wrong guy." Brianna kept talking as she walked back to her space. With no central area for people to gather or talk, we had no choice except to sit on her bed. She reached into her dresser and pulled out a very well executed colored pencil sketch of herself. Underneath it said, *to my soul mate, you rock Bri.* "I mean would a killer draw something this awesome?" she asked as she rubbed her nose with the back of her hand.

"He's very talented. You should get it framed," I suggested.

"I will, once I'm back home. I'd offer you a soda but I think Terry, one of my roommates, drank the last one."

"No problem. I'm fine." I glanced around at the surroundings. "I guess there's not much privacy for you guys when you're on the road."

She huffed and tossed her pillow behind her on the bed. "You can say that again. What brought you back here to the motorhomes?" she asked.

"Like I said, I occasionally investigate murders. Not with the police, of course. Nothing official. I sort of run a parallel investigation using my reporter's instincts and wits. I've been successful too. I'm hoping I can help make sure Cody's name is cleared." I knew I was going out on a limb, but my intuition told me Cody had nothing to do with Cherise's murder.

"That would be awesome. What can I do to help?"

"I was hoping to get a look around Cherise's things."

"The police already searched through them. Well, not really searched but they looked around. I mean it's not as if there's much to search." She waved her hand toward the front of the room.

I sat up straighter. "Do you mean Cherise bunked in here, with you?"

"Yeah, didn't you know?" she was genuinely surprised but not nearly as surprised as I was at my luck. "Her bed is the second one on the right. The one with the vintage Titanic movie poster. She had a thing for Leo."

I shrugged and smiled, thinking how cute but annoying that she considered it a vintage poster. "Leo was awfully adorable in that movie. Do you think it would be all right for me to look around her stuff? I won't mess anything up."

"I don't see why not."

I scooted through the narrow passage between the mattresses and dressers to the second bed on the right. I reached under the lampshade and turned on the light. It was a dim bulb but it gave out enough glow for me to see the space. Cherise's bed was one of the few beds that was made. It was topped with two plush velvet pillows that were decorated with gold stars, fitting decor for a fortune teller. I pulled open the top drawer. It was filled with a hairbrush, comb, hairdryer and various shampoos and soaps.

Brianna had rested back on her pillows. She was thumbing through stuff on her phone, not the slightest bit interested in my search of Cherise's belongings.

"Did you two get along well?" I asked. "Since you were room-mates and all."

Brianna peered up over her phone. "We just didn't say much to each other at all. Cherise kind of liked to keep to herself. I don't think the police found much of anything. They weren't even here for ten minutes. They took her phone but that's all."

"I suppose you all have to travel pretty lightly since you aren't given much space." I shuffled through the second drawer. It was filled with just what I would expect, clothing and socks. Her gold leather jacket was folded neatly and took up the entire bottom drawer. The leopard print boots she was wearing the night I met her at Lana's were tucked in between the mattress and the dresser. It was easy to see why the police didn't need much time to search her belongings.

"She liked to sew while we were on the road. She made those two pillows on her bed," Brianna said without looking up from her phone.

I picked up a pillow and ran my finger along the tight, neat stitching on one of the stars. "She was skilled with a needle and thread." I placed the pillow down and took a moment to look closer at the *vintage* movie poster.

It was the iconic picture of Leo and Kate standing at the ship's prow with arms outstretched. "This was such a good movie. Long but good," I noted. As I pulled my eyes away, I caught a glimpse of something white sticking out from behind the poster. It was the corner of a piece of paper.

I glanced back at Brianna. She was fully absorbed with something on her phone. I pinched the corner of the paper and gave it a little tug. A folded piece of paper slid out. As I freed it from the poster, the note fell open. A hundred dollar bill fluttered to the floor.

I stooped down and picked up the cash and read the note while I was still crouched down low enough that Brianna couldn't see what I was up to. Not that she would care either way, it seemed.

It was a piece of paper with a company letterhead, Wright Electric was written in black print across the top. The rest of the paper was blank. Not wanting to disturb any of the space, I tucked the hundred dollar bill back into the paper and slipped it behind the poster.

I stepped closer to Brianna's bed. "I'll leave you alone. I know it's been a trying day."

She looked up from her phone. "Did you find anything?"

"Not really," I lied. "I'll let my friend know about our last conversation when you told me about Cody losing his sweatshirt."

"Thanks. I hope he's back soon. I'm sure they're going to realize they made a big mistake."

"I think you're right. Take care and I'll see you later." My phone buzzed with a text as I walked out of the RV.

"I'm at the entrance," Jackson texted.

"I'll be right there."

CHAPTER 30

I saw Jackson's head above the crowd and picked up to a trot. His smile flashed white when he saw me hurrying through the maze of people.

"I think I just found another piece of evidence," I blurted as I reached him.

"Not exactly the kiss greeting I was visualizing but all right. Where is this piece of evidence?"

I took a few deep breaths to catch up after my race toward the entrance. "I was looking through Cherise's personal space, it's tiny and there isn't much there except a bed and a few clothes," I added for no real purpose except that I was still stunned by the carnies' depressing living conditions.

He crossed his arms and peered down at me with a raised brow. "And how did you manage to get into her personal space?"

"Let's just say, I've got connections." I took his arm and we headed in the direction of the hot dog stand. "Besides, shouldn't your question be—how did the investigative team miss the note and money hidden behind the Titanic poster?"

"I suppose that could have been my next question, only I knew nothing about a hidden note or a Titanic poster or anything else you're talking about."

"In my perusal of Cherise's things, I stopped to admire a Titanic poster, you know the one with Leo and Kate on the ship, and I saw the corner of a piece of paper sticking out from behind the poster. I pulled it and a hundred dollar bill fell out. It was wrapped in a blank piece of paper, only the paper wasn't completely blank. There was a letterhead printed on it, a letterhead for Wright Electric."

"Really? Huh, I'll have to let Officer Reed know. Where is it now?"

"I stuck it right back behind the poster," I said. "I didn't think it was my place to take it."

He chuckled. "Right, always following the rules."

A cluster of helium balloons caught my eye. I squeezed his arm. "There's the queen and her entourage handing out balloons," I said excitedly.

Jackson laughed. "Do you want me to get you a balloon?" he asked.

"No, they scare Redford."

"Oh, you sounded kind of thrilled to see the balloons, so I thought—"

"No, it's not the balloons. It's a theory I'm working on that has to do with Queen Melinda."

He stopped and looked at me. "What theory? What are you up to in that busy little head of yours, Bluebird?"

I squeezed his arm to keep him moving toward the hot dogs. I was starting to feel hungry too. "It's still way too crazy of a theory and with more holes than Swiss, but when it comes together into a solid block of cheese, you'll be the first to know."

"That's good. I think," he added. We reached the hot dog stand. I stayed back while he went up to order us food. I kept my eye on the cluster of balloons making its way through the crowd.

Melinda was back in her cape and crown, but her smile looked particularly forced as she handed balloons to the kids. Her three friends stayed by her side like loyal courtiers. They were making their way toward the hot dog stand. Jackson was at the window waiting for our order. I took the opportunity to chat with the entourage.

The first thing I did was glance at Melinda's left hand. Still no engagement ring. I smiled at the group. "I see the royal court has resumed," I said nicely, and got a round of smiles from the 'ladies in waiting' but not from the queen herself. "It looks like you were able to recover the queen's cape." I had to raise my voice to talk over the kids begging for balloons and the general noise of the carnival.

Confusion crossed their faces but Melinda snapped to attention. Her crown tilted forward. She pushed it hastily back. "What do you mean my cape?" There was no missing the chill in her tone.

"Oh, it's just when I saw all of you sitting by the stage, someone mentioned that you'd spent a half hour looking for it. I see now that you found it." I ended with a sweet smile. "Can't have a queen without her cape."

Like other pompous queens before her, Melinda was 'not amused'. She moved forward with her cumbersome bouquet. I needed to get in one last question. I targeted the friend who was once again wearing the jean jacket that looked almost exactly like the one I wore to school my entire sophomore year.

"Where did you eventually find the cape?" I asked her, before she walked past. Melinda was busy with her task and didn't hear me.

It took the girl a second to remember, then she spurted a laugh. "That's right. Craziest thing but Melinda found it. We were going crazy and looking all over. She said it was just sitting on a bench near one of the rides." The group got ahead of her. She raced to catch up to them before I could ask her which ride.

"Pickle relish and mustard, right?" Jackson said as I returned to the hot dog stand.

"You know you're in a serious relationship when your partner remembers your hot dog toppings." I took the skinny paper boat that was dripping with mustard and relish. "Thanks. This whole finding evidence thing is making me hungry."

Jackson looked back toward the cluster of balloons. "Was that all part of your evidence collection? Or were you just genuinely interested in balloons?"

"Definitely evidence. Let's just say I'm filling in the holes." I took a bite but it wasn't easy to do while walking.

Jackson agreed. "Let's go find a bench."

I peeked sideways at him. He was focused on finding an empty, out of the way bench.

"I'm waiting for the usual lecture about staying away from the murder investigation." I knew I was kicking the hornets' nest with my statement, but curiosity had beat out my common sense . . . yet again.

Jackson motioned toward our dining bench. We turned that direction with our paper pockets of hot dog. "No lecture this time. You're too good at this. It would be crummy and unsupportive of me to stop you in your quest to find the truth." His words were lifting my feet right off the ground, but before I could respond with a loving thank you, he stopped and turned to me. "As long as you promise, and I mean really promise, that you will let the police handle confronting the killer. No Christmastime replays. Understood?"

I saluted. "Yes, sir. No more jumping into horse carriages."

"Sunni," he said with an admonishing tone. "I'm serious."

I nodded. "I know you are and trust me, I don't want a repeat of last Christmas either." We sat down with our food. "Except maybe the dramatic kiss part. That was something I could watch on replay over and over."

"That can be arranged." He showed me his hot dog. "As you may or may not have noticed, I didn't order onions. I thought we'd take a ride on Lovers' Lane after this." He leaned forward and put his mouth close to my ear. "If the mood is right, I might even steal a kiss."

"I suppose I'll let you do that, considering you sacrificed the onions and all."

We were both hungry and made quick work of the hot dogs, then we headed in the direction of the rides. They were all in one section of the carnival. It almost didn't matter that I couldn't get out my last question about the cape. If Melinda had found it near the rides, no matter where in that area of the festivities, then she found her missing cape somewhere near the Lovers' Lane ride. Which means she *found* the cape near the very same trash can where the killer stashed Cody's blood splattered sweatshirt.

I might have filled in one or two holes, but there were still too many questions that needed answers. I knew exactly what to do next.

CHAPTER 31

There was a good long line in front of the ride, mostly giggling teens who were trying to partner up with the right 'friend' for the romantic adventure, which, in teen language, meant a place in the dark and out of the watchful eye of adults.

The Lovers' Lane ride consisted of swan shaped cars that rolled along a track, a track that led through two doors that were decorated with a large red heart. The heart split neatly in two as the doors swung open and the dingy white swans floated 'serenely' through toward whatever cheesy romantic settings awaited the passengers.

Jackson held my hand firmly in his, a habit that I'd grown fond of. I rested my head against his arm. "I'm feeling exceptionally old standing in this line."

Normally, my quip would have earned at least a chuckle, but my Lovers' Lane partner had grown unusually distracted since we'd stepped into the line.

I lifted my face to peer up at him. "Since I heard no argument to my age comment, I'll assume that you agree."

Jackson's jaw looked quite firm under the day's dark stubble as he stared ahead at a group of older teens who were especially boisterous, two guys and two girls. The kid with exceptionally greasy hair and tattoos across his knuckles was being particularly handsy with a girl, who didn't seem to mind too much. He had a deep southern accent and was throwing out the contraction *y'all* a lot.

"Jackson," I said quietly. "What has you so distracted? Or are you just reminiscing about your teenage years?"

He pulled his rapt focus away from the rowdy group and offered me what was obviously a forced smile. "It's nothing. Just watching these guys and wondering if I was as big a bozo as them. Probably," he answered himself. He squeezed my hand. "You ready for our big adventure?" The guy running the ride made an announcement that apparently carried through to the dark, walled off section of the ride. "Stay in your swan or you'll be asked to leave the carnival," he warned.

"This ride just became even less romantic," I said. "They must have cameras inside the cozy, dark areas."

"Yeah, they have to keep an eye on the inside because of people like those goofballs up there." He hadn't stopped scrutinizing the group standing a few couples ahead. Occasionally, he would lean to the side to get a better look at them. It was unusual behavior for Jackson.

"It seems that Cody is not back at the controls on this ride," I said, hoping to get his attention back. "Are they still questioning him? He didn't kill Cherise," I whispered.

Once again, he pulled his riveted gaze off the loud group and looked at me. "How do you know that?"

I shrugged. "Relying on my journalistic intuition. According to his girlfriend, Cody hardly even knew Cherise."

"Don't know if you can rely on a girlfriend as a key character witness." His gaze shot ahead. The group that had caught and held his interest was next in line for the swan cars.

I was starting to get miffed. I slowly peeled my hand away from his. "Maybe you should have just eaten the onions," I said curtly.

My sharp tone caught his attention. "Huh? Oh, sorry, it's just that—" His voice trailed off, and his body tensed as he watched the kids climb onto the ride. The loudest boy, the one with the southern drawl, climbed into the second swan with the girl.

"Sunni, prepare to be scowled at. We're going to cut in line." Jackson grabbed my hand and pulled out his badge with the free hand. He flashed it at people as he pulled me to head of the line. I picked up to a jog to keep up with his frenzied pace. He swept past the baffled, and, rightly angered, couple who were just about to step onto the ride.

Jackson held his badge out and instructed the carnie helping people onto the ride that we needed the next swan. The guy looked equally confused. More so after Jackson told him not to let anyone on the ride until we exited. People behind us groaned in protest. The carnie stood by in stunned silence as Jackson gave me a hand into the swan shaped car. He hopped in next.

It was my turn to stare at him in stunned silence but he didn't notice. He was too focused on the swan in front of us, the one that had just pushed through the two doors. The kid leaned back and yelled wahoo! His feet popped up on the side edge of the swan. He crossed one ankle over the other. The jarring movement made his sneakers glow with flickering lights.

I turned to look at him. "You have got to be kidding, Jax."

He kept his laser focus ahead as he spoke to me. "I wish I were."

The heart split open and our long necked swan floated, or, more accurately, waddled into the darkness. Twinkling lights and shiny hearts glittered overhead. A rose scented mist drifted through the air while calming music cascaded down from speakers above. Shabby carnival ride or not, it could almost have been a sweet, romantic ride, if it wasn't for the fact that my kissing partner was as coiled as a lion about to jump on prey. It was hard to keep track of the shoe lights with all the lights glittering overhead.

I was about to ask what his next move was but voices carried easily in the mostly empty room. The tail of the swan ahead of us moved along a curve on the track.

Jackson turned to me, took my face in his hands and kissed me. "Stay put." He heaved himself up and out of the swan. He swatted lights and hearts out of the way and strode past the swan directly in front of us to the next one, where the loudmouth's friend was cuddled with his girl. And there I was, alone in my swan, watching the whole thing unfold under the fragrant mist of the Lovers' Lane ride. I hadn't noticed how tightly I was holding the edge of the swan until my fingertips tingled with numbness.

"Hey, dude, you're not supposed to be walking around on this ride," the guy two swans ahead yelled at the tall figure walking next to them.

"Yeah, kind of funny to be told the rules by a *bank robber*." Jackson reached into the swan and yanked the kid out. The girl squeaked in surprise as she suddenly found herself alone in the swan as it meandered through the last turn of the ride.

Jackson had moved so fast, it took the guy with the flashy shoes a second to realize what was happening. He jumped out of the swan and ran toward the emergency exit. Jackson's foot shot out and sent the guy sailing headfirst into a bouquet of giant silk roses.

"Lights, please," Jackson yelled up to the overhead intercom.

Blinding stage lights came on and brought the entire scene into view. Both boys were stretched out on their stomachs, with hands behind their heads. Jackson stood over them with his gun pointed down.

I leaned out and looked back. The carnie had followed Jackson's order not to allow on any more passengers. The swans behind me chugged along with no riders.

Jackson pulled out his phone. "Hanson, this is Jackson. I'm

going to need both of you over at the Lovers' Lane ride," Jackson continued. "And call for some backup. We need to haul in a couple of bank robbers." Jackson winked at me as I rode past.

A few people hid smiles and giggles behind their hands as they saw me float out of Lovers' Lane alone in my swan car. The two girls who had also left the ride without their partners had already exited and stood huddled together, looking as lost and confused as two girls could be.

By the time I circled back to the front of the ride, where angry line waiters were being told the ride was closed, Officer Hanson and his partner had reached Lovers' Lane. They were communicating with Jackson as they followed the tracks through the doors and into the interior.

Fifteen minutes later, two police cars were escorted slowly through the crowd by, of all people, Calvin. They rolled up and parked behind the ride.

Jackson emerged a few minutes later looking pleased with himself. I headed toward him and gave him a hug. "I wonder how many other girls enter Lovers' Lane with big, brave boyfriends who catch bad guys in the middle of it all."

"Thought the ride needed a little more adventure," he quipped. "I think I need to follow this up with an ice cream." He took hold of my hand, and we headed toward the ice cream stand.

"How did you know for sure you had the bank robbers? I'm going to assume you didn't yank a kid out of the ride just because he was wearing flashing shoes."

"The shoes were the final detail that made me certain. A lot of the witnesses said the one guy was really loud with a Southern accent and he liked to say y'all. Like 'y'all get down on the floor and we won't shoot y'all'. Once he forgot his gloves, and the bank teller said the guy had tattoos on his knuckles. When I saw the light-up shoes, I figured I had enough to go on."

"Job well done, Detective Jackson. That is one Lovers' Lane ride I will never forget."

CHAPTER 32

I was feeling a touch giddy about my next move. My intuition told me that I was heading in the right direction for the investigation. I was so anxious to start the new day and uncover new details, I only had to hit the snooze alarm once.

Armed with my portable cup of coffee and one of Emily's banana nut muffins wrapped in a napkin, I rolled right past the newspaper office and pointed the nose of my jeep toward the Colonial Bridge and eventually the town of Smithville.

Jackson rang through on bluetooth. I tapped the screen to answer it. "Hello, handsome!"

"You sound extra cheery this morning," he said.

"Well, it's a brand new day with brand new evidence to uncover."

His deep chuckle added to the beauty of the new morning. "I wish I had your enthusiasm on cases. Maybe we should switch jobs. On second thought, scratch that. I got terrible grades in English."

"I think you'd be a great writer." I plucked my coffee cup from the cup holder and took a sip.

"I let Reed know about the money hidden behind the poster. I also wanted to let you know that they released that kid, Cody, pretty fast. His story totally checked out. Lots of people to corroborate. He was working the Lovers' Lane ride at the time of the murder. The killer must have grabbed his sweatshirt to cover his clothes and avoid blood splatter. "

"His?" I asked. "You're still thinking it's a man?"

"I think Reed was going to focus on the disgruntled ex-boyfriend next. Calvin, the maintenance man. Why? Are you leaning toward another person of interest?"

I curled my lips in trying to decide just how much I should offer. I'd solved a murder during the holiday season, only it ended in near disaster. I hadn't been able to live that tiny, harrowing fiasco down yet. I wanted to cleanly uncover the mystery and then neatly hand over the name to Jackson, without putting myself in danger. I wanted to prove to him that I could safely run my own investigation.

"Let's just say, I've got some prospects. But you'll be the first to know if I uncover anything significant."

"So, you're using me for insider information, but you're going to leave me in the dark about your next move."

"What insider information? It would've been easy enough to find out that they released Cody. I've got sources, after all."

"Of course you do. Just don't do anything—"

"Dangerous. Yes, we've been through this before, Jax. I'm going to keep my nose clear of confrontation with murderers. I promise."

There was just enough pause on his side to assure me he wasn't completely convinced. "I'm going to have to take your word for it, Bluebird. Maybe we can meet for lunch. Now that the bank robbery case is finally over, I've got a little spare time."

"That sounds good to me. I'll be hungry after all my sleuthing this morning."

A small, resigned sigh came through the speakers. "All right, P.I. Taylor, I'll call you later."

"Bye. I'll let you know if I find out anything."

The call disconnected just as I reached the big industrial building and its three smaller outbuildings. The Wright Electric logo was painted across the door fronts. My newest thread of investigation caused me to think back to that fateful day Carson discovered that Cherise had been murdered. It was only two days ago, but it felt as if weeks had passed. I'd had a few crazy busy days checking in on Lana, helping her with the business, making sure that Emily's critters were all happy and healthy and at the same time dealing with a moody ghost and my two energetic house contractors. In the chaos, I'd managed to push some inconsequential details of that day to the back of my mind. But my new theory brought them out of the shadows and moved them from inconsequential to relevant.

The carnival had started out wonderfully for Melinda. She had been crowned queen of the Spring Fair, and she had just received an apparently much anticipated proposal and diamond ring from Sutton Wright Jr., the heir to the Wright Electric company. Jackson had mentioned that Sutton senior died on the job. It was coincidentally the one day he'd gone to work without his lucky hat. The tragedy had caused Junior to become highly superstitious. Nothing about that trivial detail should have raised alarm bells when I started looking for Cherise's killer but now it was my central focus. On that same day, I was nearly run down by an anxious pair of women, both wearing the signature neon pink Wright Electric shirts, as they headed toward Cherise's tent. They seemed determined to have their fortunes told, or, at least, that was my best assessment of the situation. By the following morning, Melinda's wonderful week had gone terribly south. She was still Spring Fair Queen but the diamond ring was gone and her friends were busily trying to console her. It was easy to conclude that the engagement was off.

I parked the jeep in one of the many open spots. There were a few massive work trucks, complete with human lifts and complicated looking equipment, parked at the side of the large industrial building. It was easy to spot the office and headquarters because the name and address of the company were printed on the door.

One large desk sat in the front room of the office. There was no one sitting behind it. The walls were covered with various safety reminder posters and one of those 'days without a workplace accident' charts. It had been an impressive ninety-eight days since the last mishap. A whiteboard on the opposite wall listed job sites, locations and workers at the site. Jackson was correct. Wright Electric did a booming business.

The phone on the desk rang and footsteps hurried down a tiled hallway to the front of the office. I recognized the woman instantly as the girl I'd pegged as Sutton's sister. She looked very similar and she was close in age. The woman was surprised to see me standing inside the office. She put up her finger, letting me know she'd be right with me as she picked up the phone with her free hand.

"Wright Electric, this is Jane speaking."

I didn't want to stand rudely by and listen in on her conversation, especially because it was just a business call, so I walked over to check out the painting on the wall. Someone had masterfully executed the entire lot of Wright Electric buildings. It wasn't the most intriguing subject for artwork, but the artist had done a nice job.

"How can I help you?" Jane Wright asked as she hung up the phone. "Are you with Traver Construction?"

"No, actually, I'm with the *Junction Times*."

"I've already told Mr. Seymour that we don't need an entire page of ad space. There's already a waiting list for our services."

I stepped closer to the desk. Jane had exceptionally smooth skin and a small overbite. She also didn't seem interested in talking to me. She sat down at her desk.

"What can I do for you?" she asked. "I have a lot of work to do,"

I had formulated a plan, albeit, a weak plan, on my way to Wright Electric. With her curt attempt at a dismissal, it was getting weaker by the minute. I pulled out my pass, which she took a longer than cursory look at.

"Sunni Taylor. Yes, I've read some of your work." There was no compliment or opinion offered, which relieved and irritated me all at once. She peered up at me. "I still don't understand why you're here."

"Of course, let me explain," I added a light laugh, hoping to make her warm up. The chill continued as she leaned back and crossed her arms.

"If this is about that broken contract, that was the city's fault, not ours. The developer has already shifted his lawsuit to the city. You should go there for an interview."

It seemed she was someone who didn't mind giving out information easily. I hoped that was going to work in my favor.

"Actually, it's not about a broken contract."

Her face blanched some as she seemed to realize she'd just blurted out private company business to a local reporter. Fortunately, for her, I couldn't have cared less about a lawsuit.

"This might seem out of the blue but I'm writing an article about the Spring Fair and the Stockton Carnival."

Her mouth pulled tight. She shifted uncomfortably in her chair. "What does Wright Electric have to do with the carnival?"

"Well, I believe Sutton Wright—" I paused and squinted one eye. "Your brother, I presume, since there's a strong family resemblance."

"Yes, Sutton is my brother," she said warily, as if I was digging out some vast and explosive secret.

"I know he's engaged to the Spring Fair Queen. I was at the crowning ceremony and saw the big announcement. Congratulations on your new sister-in-law."

Her face tightened, and she squirmed even more on her chair. "Yes, well, anyhow, I have lots to do. If you don't mind." She picked up a notebook and started searching through it. I was fairly certain she was just using it as prop to show how busy she was.

"Just a quick question," I said. "I should have started with this. I'm sure you, no doubt, heard about the tragedy at the carnival." She didn't respond so I continued. She wasn't thrilled when I pulled out my notebook, but I needed my prop too. "I've decided to gather a little collection of Cherise Duvay's last fortunes. I thought it would be a nice way to pay tribute to her talents." Jane didn't look too convinced but I forged ahead. "I thought you might be able to add something to the collection."

Her mouth opened and then clamped shut and then opened again. "I—I don't understand why you're asking me."

"Oh, I'm sorry. It's just that the day before Cherise's murder, I was visiting the carnival. I just happened to see you and another woman, I think possibly your mother, walking into her tent." I motioned toward her t-shirt. "The neon pink caught my eye that day. I was standing in front of Cherise's tent when the two of you went in for your fortune. Of course, you don't have to give any specific, personal details, but in general, was it a good reading? Did Cherise say anything of note, something, as they say, providential?"

Jane seemed to be searching for a way out of the entire conversation. I half expected her just to ask me to leave the premises, but surprisingly, she opted for a logical response. It was possible she was worried about a negative comment in the paper. Sometimes the power of the press was indeed *powerful*.

"I don't go for those silly things like fortunes and card reading, but my brother enjoys learning about extra sensory perception. My mother and I thought he might enjoy having his fortune told, so we went into the tent just to make an appointment and pay in advance for his fortune. It was just sort of a gag but also something we thought he'd enjoy."

"How fun!" I said excitedly. "What a great gift idea, a way to congratulate him on his engagement. Did he have his fortune told? I would love to hear if it was good news about his future."

We were back to her squirming uncomfortably on the chair and fidgeting with the notebook. "I think she just told him some random nonsense. Those psychics have a few practiced answers for everyone to make it look real." She flipped the notebook shut and opted for the more believable prop, the telephone. "Now if you'll excuse me, I need to make some calls."

"Of course and thank you." I was out of ideas to press her on more information. I reluctantly turned and walked out of the office. I was about to rank my adventure as only a nominal success when an expensive sedan pulled into the lot. The windows were tinted so dark, it was impossible to see the driver, but when the car continued through the lot and parked in one of the reserved spots near the office, I was sure I was about to cross paths with Sutton Wright.

The door opened and Sutton climbed out of the car wearing expensive sunglasses, his neon pink shirt and carrying a leather briefcase.

"Excuse me, Mr. Wright," I said warmly.

He lifted his sunglasses. "Yes, can I help you?" His phone buzzed urgently in his hand. "Excuse me," he said. He checked the text and lifted his eyes once or twice. I caught the twinkling of a suspicious gaze. It seemed his sister had sent him a warning text about the pesky news reporter.

"I'm from the *Junction Times*." I fumbled for my pass, hoping I could salvage the situation. It would be disappointing to lose out on such a lucky opportunity.

"Yes, well, I don't have time. I'm late for a meeting." He lowered his sunglasses and strode forward, planning to sweep right past me, only luck was on my side again this morning.

"Sutton," a pleading voice called from across the lot. We both turned back toward the sound of it. Melinda was climbing out of a blue truck. She scurried on high heels toward the building. "Sutton, please, I need to talk to you."

Yep, luck wasn't just on my side. I was wearing it like a comfy, old sweatshirt.

CHAPTER 33

*M*elinda hurried across the parking lot toward Sutton. She was so focused on reaching him, she didn't seem to notice me standing there until she was just a few feet away.

"You again?" she asked.

I placed my hands against the sides of my face. "Oh my gosh, I can't believe we keep running into each other. I mean, of course we've both been hanging out at the carnival a lot so I guess that makes sense. But I never expected to see you here." I chuckled. "Although, I guess since you two are engaged, that makes sense too. I was at your crowning and I saw your announcement." I realized I was talking ridiculously fast, but a plan had popped into my head and I didn't want to lose the chance to put it into action.

I pulled my notebook and pen out while I rambled about the coincidence of seeing her again. "I hate to bother you." I shoved the notebook and pen toward her. "My ten-year-old niece has had a terrible cold all week." I looked at both of them. "Boring way to spend spring break, poor kid. But I told her I'd met the Spring Fair Queen, and she begged me to get your autograph. I would love it if

179

you could just sign this, then I promise to leave you two lovebirds alone."

She was so thrown off by my unexpected appearance and long, rambling speech, she took the paper pad in her hand. She reluctantly lifted the pen.

"Uh, her name is Stefanie—with an f," I added.

Melinda was even less friendly than our last few meetings at the carnival. She angrily dashed off an autograph and handed it back to me.

"Thank you so much. I'll leave you two alone." I headed back to my jeep, which was parked a good twenty feet away. In those twenty feet, I'd found my suspect. I stared at the notebook and the hastily written autograph.

Hey, Stefanie. Sorry you're not feeling well. Spring Fair Queen Melinda.

The f in Stefanie was not the usual grammar school, manuscript f. It had a long tail, a fancy long tail, just like the f written in blood on Cherise's mirror.

I hadn't even reached my jeep before Melinda jumped into an emotional conversation with Sutton. In a low hushed tone, he suggested they take it inside but she screamed no.

"I can't go inside. I can't be in the same building with your mom and sister," she said loudly enough to make sure people inside heard her.

I slowly climbed into my jeep, turned the key and rolled down the window on the passenger side, the side where the heated conversation was taking place. It wasn't like me to tape a personal conversation but something told me, I needed to record it.

"I blamed that woman at the carnival, that fake fortune teller." Melinda waved her hands around and then crossed them. She paced around in a short circle before stopping in front of Sutton.

He looked as if he wanted to melt into the sidewalk or, at the very least, vanish into thin air.

"How could you believe something so silly?" she asked. "Everyone knows those psychics are fake but not Sutton Wright," she yelled. "The head of a big company but a complete stranger warns him that he's about to make the biggest mistake of his life and he breaks off his engagement." She smacked his chest and, obviously, feeling rightly ashamed, Sutton took it. "Then I find out it wasn't the fortune teller at all. It was those two conniving women, your mom and sister, who paid the fortune teller to lie. That's how badly they wanted to break us up, and it worked because you are a fool!" She screamed, then spun around and covered her face.

Her dramatic scene seemed to be working. Sutton looked sympathetic toward her, almost as if he was thinking he'd made a terrible mistake breaking off the engagement. I couldn't see inside the office, but something told me his sister, Jane, was looking on in horror at the scene outside.

I stopped recording and opened up a text box to Jackson. "I know who killed Cherise but don't worry, I'm safe in my jeep. You might want to watch this video. It sort of tells the whole story. And I was right about the bloody message on the mirror. It was a woman's writing." I clicked send and drove my jeep out of the lot.

Sutton might have been thinking it was time to patch things up with his betrothed, but I was pretty sure that was not going to happen.

I was only a block away from Wright Electric when Jackson called.

"You are amazing," he said as I answered.

"Why, thank you," My face warmed at the compliment.

"I know Officer Reed had been focused on Ivonne and Cherise's ex-boyfriend. How did you figure out it was the Spring Fair Queen?" he asked.

"I didn't at first. That handwriting sample was my best piece of evidence since I didn't get to see anything else the police collected. I was focused on Ivonne, the jealous wife. I even found a note she'd written to Cherise telling her to stay away from Carson or she'd be fired. It was her final warning, she wrote. The f on final wasn't elongated, which made me wonder if I was looking in the wrong direction. Calvin, the head of maintenance and the broken hearted ex-boyfriend, was my second person of interest. But his f didn't match either. I saw his handwritten to-do list for a coworker. Then there was the hidden hundred dollar bill, which just happened to be folded into a piece of paper with the Wright Electric letterhead. And that's where *you* come in."

"Me? What did I do?" he asked.

"You told me the story about Sutton Wright and his lucky hat and how his death made his son superstitious. Also, Melinda's friends, who I'm sure knew nothing about the murder, mentioned in a casual conversation with me that they had to look all over for her seemingly lost red cape. Guess where they finally found it?"

"Outside the Lovers' Lane ride where Melinda switched the cape for Cody's sweatshirt?"

"Bingo."

"I'm going to call Officer Reed right now and see where she's at on the case. She's not going to be thrilled that she fell behind a reporter on this, but you really deserve the credit. Good job."

"Thanks. Guess I deserve a lunch."

"You sure do. Should we meet at Layers at noon?"

"Sounds good. This detective stuff has really made me work up an appetite."

CHAPTER 34

*I*t was as if the sun had come out to warm and brighten the cherry red picnic benches in front of Layers just to make the day even better. Jackson was running a few minutes late, so I'd ordered the Valentino for him, a fitting sandwich for the man, and I had landed on the Chaplin, with its layers of peppery arugula and turkey. Layers had so many glamorously named sandwiches and salads, it was usually hard to decide, but the Chaplin had popped right off the menu at me so the choice was easy.

The triplet tulip poplars that shaded the eating area were heavy with sumptuous pink blossoms, and birds seemed to be twittering at me from every direction. I had to resist the urge to whistle a tune right along with my feathery troubadours. A dash of guilt hit as it occurred to me, while basking in my glory, that I hadn't checked in on Lana for a day. She had been avoiding texting, claiming it was laborious with one hand, so I rang her up.

"Hey, Sunni, what's new?" she blurted before I could ask her the same.

I was more than willing to talk about myself. "Well, let's see. I'm about to have a Chaplin at Layers with my favorite detective. I'm just waiting for him to show up. Ursula and Henry are lining up a guy to restore the wood shelving in the library. Oh, and I solved the murder of Cherise Duvay."

"Yahoo! You should have been a private investigator. Who was it? The jealous wife?"

"Nope, I'll tell you all about it later. I've got to wait for confirmation from Jackson that they've made the arrest. Just in case, on the crazy off chance that I have the wrong suspect."

She laughed. "Did you have to take a harrowing carriage ride to find this one?"

"Nope. I kept my nose clear of danger. How is your wrist?" Jackson pulled up to the curb.

"It's still broken, unfortunately."

"Let me know if you need me to do anything for the party. I wrote my article in just two hours, so I've got some free time." Jackson climbed out of his car. "Lana, I'll have to talk to you later. There is an extraordinarily handsome man walking toward me with a pink bakery box in his hands. One of the best sights I've ever laid eyes on, especially if my favorite chocolate mocha cupcakes are inside the box."

"I'll let you go, then," Lana said. "Say hello to the extraordinarily handsome man for me."

I hung up and couldn't stop myself from skipping toward him for a quick hug and to help with his bakery burden. "Lana says hello." I took a strong whiff of the box. "Do I smell chocolate mocha?"

He stopped. "Is *that* the kind you like? I bought you their new sugarless prune cupcakes."

I blinked up at him, clutching the box against me. "I hope you're kidding."

His face broke instantly into a smile. "I had you there for a second." He leaned forward and kissed me. "That bottom lip was just starting to jut forward in a pout at the words *sugarless* and *prune*."

"Who wouldn't pout at those words? They should be stricken from the language." I headed back to the table with the box. "I ordered the Valentino, just like you asked," I said as I slid onto the red bench. "Isn't it a beautiful, fantastic day?" I swept my arms around to point out the trees, sun and birds for visual proof.

Jackson was suppressing a grin as he tossed his long legs over the bench and sat down. "Someone is happy about catching a killer," he noted.

I leaned forward and rested my forearms on the table. The shiny red surface was hot under the midday sun. "So—did I catch one? Did Melinda kill Cherise?"

"According to her very tear-filled confession, she was so out of her mind with heartbreak she didn't know what she was doing. Of course, she was still in a solid enough state of mind to plan out pulling someone else's sweatshirt on over her clothes to avoid blood splatter. Sutton was the ignorant fool in all this. His sister and mom confessed to paying for an arranged fortune telling session for Sutton where Cherise would inform him that his engagement was a terrible mistake. Apparently, they had never approved of the relationship."

I sat back feeling even more excited. My entire theory had proved correct. "Maybe they had something there," I said. "After all, not that many people would resort to murder and a particularly heinous one at that. What's ridiculous is that Sutton actually allowed a carnival fortune teller to change his mind about his engagement."

"True. That was ridiculous."

The server brought out our food. My stomach churned in anticipation.

I picked up the sandwich. "This crime solving stuff sure makes me hungry. I've been snacking on Myrna's pistachio nuts all morning and I'm still starved."

We ate in silence for a few minutes, both of us enjoying our sandwich choices and iced teas. I finally worked up the courage to ask about Officer Reed's reaction to my barging in on the case. "Was Officer Reed upset that I'd been searching out clues for the murder?"

He nodded as he finished a bite of food, then took a drink of tea. "I think her pride took a small hit, but she's great at her job. It seemed your last clue, the money behind the poster had opened up a new lead for the team. They were heading to Wright Electric next to find out the story behind the money. I'm sure the officer who searched through Cherise's meager belongings is going to get an earful about missing it in the first place. They were just glad to wrap the case up so quickly." He winked at me. "Which is all because of you, Bluebird."

I wriggled my bottom and sat up straighter. "I *am* proud of myself, thanks. So proud that I might stop halfway between this sandwich and eat one of those cupcakes because I deserve it."

"You certainly do. I guess you've got a 'killer', no pun intended, article for the paper. Chase is going to get another kick in the seat, eh?"

I hadn't even thought about Chase when I sat down to write my mundane, vapid story about the carnival. "I'm afraid it won't be a kick at all. I sat at my desk for the longest time, fingers poised and mind racing with all the gritty, newsworthy details, but I couldn't do it. Cherise lost her life for such a shallow, ludicrous reason, and Melinda's life is ruined. One moment she's being crowned Spring Fair Queen and gushing to everyone that she is engaged to one of the town's most eligible bachelors, and the next, she's posing for a mug shot and searching for a defense lawyer. It was all too sad to write about. I just wrote a nice, nostalgic piece about the carnival. Parker will probably blow his stack, and Chase will wear a nasty smirk for the next month. But in the end, I think I did the right thing."

"I think so too." Jackson's amber eyes glittered like gold in the sunlight as he gazed at me with a look that warmed me from head to toe. Without pulling his eyes from my face, he reached for the box, opened it and lifted out a frosting laden cupcake. "Here's a sweet for my sweet, the best darn journalist slash detective this side of the Smokies. And probably the other side too."

CHAPTER 35

$\mathcal{T}$he excitement of the day had finally caught up to me. I was tired and wide yawns intercepted each deep breath. I absently tapped the cup of hot tea sitting in front of me as I stared down at the envelope sitting on the table next to the tea. I had planned to open it in my bedroom, to read it in private, and if the news wasn't great, I could just not tell him. But after our last conversation, Edward made it clear he wanted to know more about his son, James. I wasn't sure that the information inside had anything to do with his son, but I surmised that it had something to do with Bonnie Ross, or Milton.

"Well, what are you waiting for," Edward's voice carried across the room. "Neither of us is getting any younger," he quipped.

"Yes but only one of us is getting older, and according to the tiny lines next to my eyes, that is me." I peered back over my shoulder in the direction of his voice. He was leaning casually against the doorjamb with his arms crossed over his untied cravat as if whatever was in the envelope meant very little to him. Only I knew that wasn't true.

"You're sure about this?" I asked.

"I'm not unsure so I must be sure. If that makes sense."

I lifted the envelope. "Not really but here goes." I carefully opened the envelope. It was very likely one of the last ones Henrietta Suffolk had filled. I pulled free the papers folded inside. The last sheet was a clean piece of paper folded over two older pieces of faded parchment. The printed ink on each piece of parchment was still fresh and clear, but the handwritten parts of the documents were faded and hard to read. One was a marriage certificate and one was a birth certificate. Tucked inside the entire set of pages was a half sheet of paper, a handwritten letter from Henrietta Suffolk. The writing was shaky and a little hard to read. I could only imagine how much effort it took her to write.

Edward was watching me from across the room. Normally, he had no qualms about reading something over my shoulder, but he stayed a safe distance away waiting patiently to hear the news about his son.

I held up the note. "It's from Henrietta Suffolk, the woman who is a direct descendant of the family who took Bonnie in after Cleveland sent her away. Shall I read it?"

His nod was ever so slight.

I cleared my throat and read slowly for him to hear every word.

Dear Miss Taylor,

I understand you are the present owner of the Cider Ridge Inn. I'm afraid my eyesight is failing but I wanted to send these documents because I feel they are connected to the legacy of the inn. I'm a direct descendant of Carlson Suffolk, a distant cousin of Cleveland Ross, the man who built your home. An affair and a tragic duel left Cleveland's young wife pregnant and without a home. Cleveland asked Carlson to take her in. I am unable to find the birth certificate, but according to stories passed down through

*the generations, Bonnie gave birth to James Henry Milton in fall
of 1817.*

I looked up. Edward had drifted closer. "That matches up with
the birth certificate I found in the records office," I noted, but it
was hard to know if he was paying attention. His gaze was riveted
on the letter so I continued.

*By all accounts, James was a happy, smart and enjoyable boy who
grew up to attend college and eventually earn a law degree. He
was very loyal to the Suffolk family, for he had no other relatives
or family ties. Young Bonnie never spoke much about his father. It
was too difficult to talk about. Bonnie died of a fever just a few
days after James entered law school, so, more than ever, he turned
to his 'adopted' family, the Suffolks. In the envelope, I've included
a marriage certificate dated April 4th, 1837. On that day, James
Henry Milton married Clarissa Moore, a wealthy banker's
youngest daughter. In addition, I've sent you a copy of a birth
certificate for their first born, a daughter named Mary Virginia
born in 1842. I'm afraid this is where the trail ends on my side.
James and Clarissa moved to Ohio for James's law practice. They
wrote often at first, but as time passed and their lives got busy, the
correspondences slowed. I hope this gives a little insight into the
woman who once lived in your house.*

Sincerely,
Henrietta Suffolk

I sighed. "How sad that I'm not going to be able to thank her for
taking the time to write and send the certificates." I lifted my eyes
from the letter.

Edward was standing close by staring down at the documents

on the table. "A lawyer," he said, "an admirable profession." There was a hitch in his usually fluid tone.

"It certainly is." I picked up the birth certificate. "And he had a daughter. You're a grandfather. I can do more research to find out what happened to Mary Virginia, but only if you want me to. Otherwise, I'll stop looking."

His face popped up. "You can't stop now. Do you stop a chapter before the end of a book? I want to know. Don't you?"

I laughed. "Yes. Yes, I do."

ABOUT THE AUTHOR

London Lovett is the author of the Firefly Junction, Port Danby and Starfire Cozy Mystery series. She loves getting caught up in a good mystery and baking delicious new treats!

Subscribe to London's newsletter [londonlovett.com] to never miss an update.

You can also join London for fun discussions, giveaways and more in her *Secret Sleuths* Facebook group.

https://www.facebook.com/groups/londonlovettssecretsleuths/

Instagram @LondonLovettWrites

https://www.londonlovett.com/
londonlovettwrites@gmail.com

Made in the USA
Las Vegas, NV
02 March 2023

68388907R00114